A THEFT OF HONOUR

Who was he, this self-styled Colonel
Thomas Blood? Troublemaker, Irish up-
start, unscrupulous rogue, or one of the
most loyal subjects Charles II could wish
for? He certainly became notorious during
the years of the Restoration for his
conspiracies, intrigues and – his most daring
feat – the theft of the Crown Jewels.

Court Life vies with political intrigue as
destiny leads Kate Varney, a young maid
rescued by Blood from a Dublin riot, into
the arms of Tom Hunt, his second-in-
command. This is a dangerous romance, for
Tom's future is bound up with one of the
most daring criminals in English history...

For
Stella
my *guiding star*

A THEFT
OF HONOUR

by

Aileen Armitage

Magna Large Print Books
Long Preston, North Yorkshire,
BD23 4ND, England.

British Library Cataloguing in Publication Data.

Armitage, Aileen
    A theft of honour.

A catalogue record of this book is
available from the British Library

ISBN   0-7505-1631-3

First published in Great Britain in 2000 by
Severn House Publishers Ltd.
Originally published 1972 under the title *Bloodstone* and
pseudonym *Aileen Quigley*.

Copyright © 1972 by Aileen Quigley
Copyright © 2000 by Aileen Armitage

Cover illustration © Len Thurston by arrangement with
P.W.A. International Ltd.

The moral right of the author has been asserted

Published in Large Print 2001 by arrangement with
Severn House Publishers Ltd.

Magna Large Print is an imprint of Library Magna Books Ltd.

Printed and bound in Great Britain by
T.J. (International) Ltd., Cornwall, PL28 8RW

ONE

Inside the grey stone walls of Dublin Castle the Duke of Ormond, Lord Lieutenant of Ireland, waited to be attacked. He stretched his velvet-breeched legs towards the fire and leaned back leisurely in his high-backed chair. His visitor, Sir Theophilus Jones, watched him from a courteous distance and wondered how he could treat the affair with such apparent indifference.

'There is no cause to alarm yourself, I assure you,' Ormond said calmly. 'His Majesty the King and I have endured far greater threats in the past, alone and undefended by guards, when we wandered Europe together, penniless, in the bad old days. An uprising now by a band of Irish discontents perturbs me but little.'

His lazy drawl and his casual manner irritated Sir Theophilus, for it was at no little risk to his safety that he had brought warning to the Duke of the danger that threatened, and Ormond seemed to be treating the matter as if it were of no more

5

consequence than a village maypole dance.

'But these are no mere peasants, my lord,' he protested, waving his arms so agitatedly that the sleeves of his black robe flapped like a scarecrow in a windswept field. 'Ever since His Majesty was so fortunately restored to his throne, many of the most powerful Cromwellians have banded together to try to regain their lost lands and rights. The committee of men which leads them conspires here in Dublin, right under your very eminent nose, men like Thomas Blood and his brother-in-law, Leckie, confirmed Presbyterians and gallant soldiers both.'

'I know, I know.'

'And I had the information of a most reliable source, my lord, a member of the committee himself, who sought to do himself a good turn by selling the information. The plotters intend to seize both the castle and yourself, my lord, and heaven alone knows what they may do to you, such malice they bear the English government.'

Ormond rose from his chair and crossed to the latticed window. He stood thoughtfully, watching the main gate overhung by beech trees now full in leaf, and the crowds of peasants and housewives, pedlars and merchants hurrying to and fro.

'You will observe, Sir Theophilus, that I have doubled the guard since you brought me this news. I have also seen to it that troops and militia have been called out, and the other nearby districts have been warned. Blood and Leckie and their friends will find a lively reception prepared for them on the day. But tell me, exactly how do they propose to enter the castle?'

Sir Theophilus brightened at the thought of being in a more knowing position than the Lord Lieutenant for the moment. He spread his hands expressively.

'Everyone knows my lord receives petitions every day, in the main hall where any curious person has access. They plan to send some of their members inside, claiming to be petitioners, while as many as eighty or a hundred more hang about outside, pretending to be workmen or merely loiterers. Philip Arden – that's the committee member I spoke of – tells me that one of them, dressed as a baker, will enter the castle carrying a tray of freshly-baked loaves, but just as he enters the main gate, he will trip and fall, letting his loaves roll on the ground. They hope the guards will leap on them eagerly, fighting will break out, and in the confusion the plotters will surge in, their confederates inside having opened the doors to them.'

'My guards will not scavenge for dusty loaves,' Ormond commented quietly. 'They are too well-disciplined. But let them try their manoeuvre. On the tenth of the month, you say?'

'That is so, my lord.'

Ormond sat down again, waved his hand as a sign of dismissal, and Sir Theophilus bowed and left the chamber. Ormond sat rubbing the side of his nose thoughtfully with a tanned, weatherbeaten finger that spoke of the many long years he had spent out of doors as a soldier.

After a few minutes there was a scuffle outside the door, voices rising and pro-testing, and then the door opened suddenly and Sir Theophilus, red-faced and eager, rushed in again.

'My lord, pardon my informality,' he prattled breathlessly, making a faint sem-blance of a sketchy bow, 'but I found this Philip Arden awaiting me below.'

'So?' Ormond's bushy eyebrows rose in question.

'The plotters know – and have changed their plan.'

'Know what, sir?'

'They know that you know, my lord, that you have been warned of their attack.'

'So they have abandoned it, is that it?'

'No, no, my lord.' Sir Theophilus' eyeballs were protruding brightly in his excitement. He glanced agitatedly towards the window. 'They have changed only the date – to the fifth.'

'The fifth?' Ormond's voice was incredulous. 'Why, that's today!' Instantly the Duke's lazy air vanished. He rose from his chair and strode purposefully to the door. A lifetime's training in making instant decisions to meet imminent danger was apparent in his cool, swift orders to the sentry at the door, and then Ormond disappeared. Sir Theophilus decided he would stay up here in the safety of the tower and watch events from the window. After the frustration of the plotters he knew he would be well rewarded for his trouble.

Outside the grey walls of Dublin Castle a little girl moved among the crowd, searching for the arm of her beloved rag doll. Poor Mopsy, she looked so dejected and awry, with a gaping hole where her arm should be, and the stuffing falling loose. But it would be almost impossible to find it under all

9

these feet shuffling through the dust on their way to or from the market. And it was the dust that was making her eyes smart, Kate told herself firmly, not tears. Big girls don't cry.

She walked closer to the main gates of the castle, her eyes fixed on the ground. She had walked this way earlier, she remembered, so it was just possible that the poor little arm could be lying here somewhere. She hugged poor Mopsy close to her thin chest, to comfort and reassure her.

Suddenly voices began shouting nearby. A soldier cried in a very loud voice, 'The baker, he's here, captain!' and Kate looked up in alarm. A man carrying a tray of loaves on his head as he approached the castle gate looked startled, threw down his tray so that the crisp loaves scattered in every direction, and turned and fled. People everywhere cried out in pleasant surprise and fell on the bread, anxious to claim one of the abandoned loaves as booty. Then distant hoofbeats began to echo down the street, guards carrying muskets marched out of the castle gates, people shrieked and ran, and the hoofbeats thundered nearer.

Kate suddenly leapt forward, unaware of the noise. Not for a loaf, though, hungry as she was, but for the lost little arm, lying just there, outside the castle gate. Glory be to God, thought Kate in delight, Mopsy would be whole again!

Just as she snatched the arm up eagerly from the dust, a big black bird seemed to swoop on her from out of the sky. It carried her up in the air and away, the breath almost squeezed from her body. Hoofbeats thundered by and a swish of warm, dusty air hurtled past her, then she was flying down a maze of side streets, held tight and uncomfortably against what she at last realised was a man's hard, warm, panting body. Someone tried to bar his way and he cried out loudly, 'Let me take my child away from harm, in God's name, man! Fighting is no place for a little one!'

The bodies fell away and the man ran on, stopping only at last when his breath was being drawn in huge, sobbing gasps. He set Kate down and leaned his height against the whitewashed wall of a cottage, clutching his side as though in pain. Kate rubbed her sore ribs gingerly, and then Mopsy's too, for she was sure to have been crushed as Kate was. Mercifully the lost arm was still in Kate's hand.

The man, doubled almost in half and

11

drawing enormous, noisy gulps of air, at length began to breathe more quietly. He was tall and had very black hair, Kate saw, and with his black cloak as well it was not surprising she had mistaken him for a big black crow. He was watching her now, an amused curve on his lips and his eyes as dark as any crow's but far gentler and more kindly. They were nice eyes, Kate thought, laughing and gay, even if his nose was rather fat and ugly.

'Why did you grab me so roughly?' she enquired. The man's eyebrows lifted.

'Was I rough? Then forgive me, mistress, for so fair a maid should be treated gently. I had no wish to hurt you, but did you not see the soldiers on horseback coming? You would have been crushed under their hooves for sure, so swiftly you darted forward. Would you be wanting to get yourself crushed so?'

'I found Mopsy's arm,' Kate explained, holding the mutilated member aloft for him to see. The man took it and examined it politely. Kate could not help but notice what a huge thumb he had on his right hand, twice as big as the other, but she did not comment. The man gave her back Mopsy's arm.

'I am sure you must be very pleased to have found it, but take care another time, little one, or I may not be there to grab you.'

'Why were you there?'

The man considered a moment. 'Let us say it was the hand of God, child. I was sent to that spot at that very moment to see your danger. When you go home, offer a prayer of thanks to God for your deliverance. I too must thank you.'

'Me?' said Kate in surprise. 'Why?'

'Having you under my arm saved me from the militia who would have arrested me in the lane for sure, but that they believed me to be a terrified father running with his child. I shall always remember my pro-tectress.' His eyes shone with amusement as he spoke. 'Tell me how you are called, little one?'

'Kate Varney. And you?'

His eyes darkened momentarily, and then flickered into life again. He doffed his hat and swept her a flourishing bow.

'Mistress Varney – Colonel Thomas Blood, at your service.'

Kate was entranced. She had received the first, beautiful, gentlemanly bow in all her nine years of life. She drew herself up to her full height.

13

'Farewell, Kate – and my thanks,' the man said softly. 'I must go now, and quickly.'

'And I too,' Kate said gravely, 'for I plan to go to see the strolling players this evening if my mammy will give me a groat.'

'Away with ye, you spalpeen,' he roared with laughter, and when Kate turned at the corner to glance back, he was gone. She walked back towards the town as in a trance. Her first, gallant bow! And from a gentleman with such eyes! She would remember those eyes all her life. And the gentleman – what was his name? Blood, ugh! It was a horrid name, but the tall, dark, kindly man she knew she would never forget.

Ormond drummed his fingers impatiently on the smooth surface of the vast oak writing table. He looked up when a tap came at the door and an officer entered and saluted him.

'Well?' Ormond's voice was a sharp, peremptory bark.

'We have arrested a number of them, my lord, but many escaped in the crowd.'

'Who amongst them, captain? Have you Leckie and Blood, or any of the other leaders?'

'Leckie is below, my lord, cursing and swearing like no minister I have ever heard before. And a number more.'

'And Blood?' Ormond's eyes pierced the young captain's. 'He is the danger – have you caught him?'

'I regret not, my lord. If he were there at all, he must have eluded us.'

'Of course he was there!' Ormond retorted sharply. 'Blood is always at the forefront of any fray. Despite his mischief he is a man of courage, I'll grant him that.'

He stood silent then, musing and tapping his fingers on the desk again. The young officer coughed and murmured, 'Your orders, sir?'

Ormond straightened. 'Imprison them all. Clap Leckie in irons. Interrogate him closely to discover the names and whereabouts of his associates, and tell me what you find out. We must, at all costs, find and render harmless this nest of old Cromwellians. That is all.'

The young man saluted and turned to go. As he opened the door Ormond added, 'There is no need to deal gently with Leckie, captain. I must have the information he possesses. One way or another I am determined to bring Blood to justice.'

The officer nodded briefly and withdrew.

But early summer in Dublin grew into high midsummer and then faded into autumn mists, and still Ormond fumed that he had made no progress. Leckie lay in his cell, half-dead from the treatment he had received and quite out of his scholarly mind, but still he obdurately refused to speak. The fellow's wife had pleaded repeatedly for his release, and even the Fellows of Trinity College, whose colleague Leckie was, had begged for his life, but Ormond remained firm. If the fellow conformed, and told what he knew, it would have been another matter, for capturing Blood was the prime pre-occupation in Ormond's mind, but Leckie was stubborn. Very well then, let him rot and the devil take him for his obstinacy!

One moonlit autumn evening a grey-robed figure stole silently across Dublin and knocked at the door of a cottage. Mrs Leckie, who was about to extinguish the candles and go to bed, looked up in surprise. She opened the door cautiously, and was astounded to see a Catholic priest on her doorstep – and she a convinced Presbyterian too, wife of a Presbyterian minister!

'What can I do for you, Father?' she asked

him politely enough, but there was coolness in her voice. She had too much to worry over, with her dear husband languishing in prison in fear of his life, to concern herself overmuch with a begging friar.

'Whisht, alannah,' a soft voice urged from under the cowl. 'Open the door wider and let me pass before I am seen.'

'Thomas!' she cried, recognising the voice of her brother and stepping aside to let him in. 'It is not safe for you to be here!'

She closed and locked the door quickly behind him. 'Dear God, Tom, you should not be here! The soldiers come often to search for Dissenters and ask me questions. They may be watching the house now.'

'Tell me the news quickly,' Blood answered urgently. 'Your husband – is he still captive? Is he well?'

His sister pressed her finger to her lips. 'Let not the children hear you, Tom. They are abed but they will recognise your voice instantly and come running.'

'But Leckie – have they harmed him?'

She hung her head. 'They have treated him most cruelly, but he bears it all with fortitude. Several of the leaders have already been sentenced and have lost either liberty or property or both. But I fear many are soon to lose their lives, and mayhap my Leckie amongst them. And you, brother, have been declared an outlaw with a price upon your head. Your lands have been confiscated too. There is naught to keep you in Ireland now, Tom. Why do you not go abroad, to England or to Holland?'

'I cannot leave you at a time like this, but if I stay I can think of no way to help. I cannot attempt to rescue Leckie unaided; not from the castle dungeons, in any event.'

'You can do nothing alone, now most of your colleagues have been taken,' his sister replied firmly, 'and I do not expect it. I am grateful that Leckie remains steadfast and loyal, and if he is to lose his life, I shall be proud of him for his courage and loyalty.'

'But the children,' Blood mourned. 'Your children will be deprived of their father. I must think of some plan to help him. A rescue – on the way to the scaffold, mayhap, if it should come to that.'

'Alone?'

'I am in correspondence with other Non-Conformists in Ulster and Scotland and Lancashire. I may be able to enlist their help. We shall see.'

Blood took off his grey robe wearily and sank into the chair by the fire. The light from the fire gleamed on his dark hair and revealed the haggard, hollow look of his eyes.

'Let me give you food,' his sister said, her maternal feelings aroused by his tired, defeated appearance. She bustled towards the kitchen.

'Aye, food, and a little rest methinks, and then before dawn I must be on my way again. There is work to be done,' Blood murmured sleepily, and by the time his sister returned with a tray of cold meat and a tankard of ale he was soundly asleep by the fire.

In the morning he was gone. Autumn mists in Dublin thickened into November fogs, and in vain the Duke of Ormond continued to search for the elusive Colonel Blood. Not a trace of him was to be discovered in Dublin or for miles around. It was almost as if the man had vanished into the air like a ghost, leaving no trace.

By now he must have escaped safely abroad, Ormond decided. There was no point in delaying the execution of the remaining committee members any longer, in the hope of drawing Blood out into the open. They must all die, Leckie amongst them.

Leckie. Ormond's conscience twinged just a little over the man. He had subjected the fellow to abominable treatment with the result that he was now completely mad, but Ormond had sworn never to let him go if he remained silent, not until he handed over the body to Leckie's wife. And so it should be.

The execution was planned for a day in early December. All round Dublin tongues clacked and the rumour grew from nowhere that the amazing Colonel Blood would sweep into the town on the day of the execution and carry off his brother-in-law from the very brink of death. Woe betide anyone who stood in Blood's way, they said, and silently every citizen vowed that he at least would keep well clear of the market place on that day.

Little Kate Varney heard her father telling her mother about it as he put more peat turves on the low fire in the kitchen. Her eyes grew round with surprise. The ruthless, daring soldier they were speaking of, Colonel Blood, did they say? Why, that was how her dark-eyed friend was named. It could not be the same man!

So she asked her father about the man the Lord Lieutenant was seeking. How did he look?

'The description of the man they seek says he is tall, has dark hair and dark eyes and a long, broad nose. And he is aged about forty-five,' her father told her. 'But even if he does reappear to save his friend, we shall not be there to see, little one, for he is fierce and cruel and we shall stay clear of the town that day.'

Kate kept silent. The description did indeed sound like her friend, save that he was neither fierce nor cruel. But she would not argue with her father. In any event, Mother would be cross with her for not telling her of the man who had pulled her from the Castle gates. Mother was always cross if she spoke to strangers. She would be unlikely to believe that the man had saved her from the horses' hooves, especially if he was Colonel Blood, the ogre who terrified everyone.

The day of the execution came, chill and grey with rain. The market place was empty save for a few brave souls, and they were doomed to disappointment, for no avenging black figure swooped down to wrest the prisoner from the hangman's grasp as they had hoped. Leckie died quietly, and the townsfolk mourned that the hated Duke had not been cheated of his victory.

Afterwards the lifeless body, white and flaccid after months of being imprisoned underground, was duly handed over to Mistress Leckie as Ormond had promised.

Some nights later, the widow sat alone in her cottage, her eyes dry and her heart heavy with unshed tears. A knock at the door aroused her from her torpor, and she opened it to find the priest who had come in the night months before.

'Let me pass.' He was inside before she could speak.

'Tom, oh Tom!' She buried her face in the rough cloth of his cassock and at last the tears flowed. For some minutes she sobbed unrestrainedly into his shoulder, and his big brown hand patted her reassuringly. At length she stood back, dabbing her eyes with her apron, and looked at him. His face was rigid with determination.

'I shall see to you, alannah, and to the children, have no fear on that score,' he said roughly. She nodded. She knew he would. 'But Ormond shall pay for this, I swear,' he added, his voice low and hissing with menace.

'No, Tom, there is no need for revenge,' his sister murmured. 'It is not Christian.'

'Christian or no, I swear to you here and

now that I shall avenge Leckie's death. Sooner or later Ormond will pay. It may take me a lifetime, sister, but one day I shall have Ormond at my mercy, and this I promise you.'

Before she could protest, the door had opened and closed behind him. She looked out of the latticed window into the night, but shadows flitting under the moonlight made it impossible for her to distinguish which shadow might be the grey-robed figure of a priest.

She sighed and went back to sit by the fire.

TWO

The years slipped by, slowly for a little girl who lived close by the walls of Dublin Castle and who was anxious to grow into a woman, and swiftly for the Duke of Ormond, Lord Lieutenant of Ireland, who felt that age was overcoming him before he could accomplish all that his youthful vigour had set out to do.

During that time little was seen of the notorious Colonel Blood in Ireland, though news of his escapades filtered through, first to the frustrated ears of Ormond, and eventually, much later, to the fascinated ears of little Kate Varney, hovering on the brink of womanhood. Rumour had it that he no longer stayed in Ireland, his confiscated estates having been given to a Captain Toby Barnes, but flitted silently from England to the Continent and back, leaving a trail of dissension in his wake.

But Kate had many other pressing problems to occupy her mind, her struggling parents finding it difficult to find food enough for themselves and their one surviving child in these days of hardship. Reluctantly they put Kate to work in a gentleman's residence as a kitchen maid, and for her at least life became easier.

She was treated well enough for a maidservant, and when the plague that had smitten London a year earlier found its way into Ireland and robbed her of both parents, Kate was already thirteen. Her employers, the Lennies, had removed their entire household into the country until the danger was over, and when Kate came back with them to Dublin she hastened gladly to see her parents again. She found their little cottage deserted. The door swung idly in the breeze and the leaves blew around the brick floor of the kitchen. Neighbours broke the news to her as gently as they could, of how they had found Patrick and his faithful Kathleen dead of the plague, entwined in each other's arms. Kate was alone in the world now.

She went back to the little garret in the Lennie's house that was assigned to her and Bridget, another kitchen maid, and sobbed for a whole week together. Bridget watched her uncomfortably as she lay weeping on the truckle bed, and kept wiping her own nose on her sleeve from time to time. She was obviously near to tears herself in sympathy with her friend. Suddenly Bridget sat upright.

'I know, Kate! Let's go down to see the strolling players! I know you always had a liking for a play, and they're doing one in the old barn down the Cork road. Come now, dry your eyes and let's be going.'

Kate sat up slowly, wiping her face with the hem of her gown. The players. Bridget was right. Kate loved to see the players in their gaudy tinsel costumes, looking like real kings and queens under the flashing torchlight. And the mistress had given them both the evening off, so if she and Bridget had enough money between them, where was the harm in seeking a little diversion?

As she splashed her face and brushed her hair she felt a little guilty. Patrick and Kathleen had never approved of hard-earned pence being squandered on watching the mummers, but they had always smiled indulgently and let her go in the end if the groat could be found. After so many tears shed in their memory, Kate hoped they would approve her going now.

It was a fine, starlit night as Kate and Bridget walked home along the country lanes after the play had ended. Kate sang as she walked, holding her head erect and mimicking the queen in the play. Bridget chuckled in amusement.

'I saw a young fellow there who had his eye on you the whole time, Kate,' she commented enviously. Kate nodded and went on humming. 'It was one of the actors, the one who offered his life to the gods,' Bridget went on. 'His eyes were on the audience the whole time he was speaking – on you, Kate.'

Kate walked forward a few steps, turned and struck a dramatic pose, her arms outstretched and her face turned up to the stars. 'Oh Bridget!' she breathed ecstatically,

'I should like above all things to be an actress. To wander from town to town, to wear fine clothes and have everyone come to see and admire! Oh, what a wonderful life they lead!'

Bridget snorted. 'Actress, indeed! I'll wager it's not half such a fine life as you think, Kate. Cold and half-starving half the time, I'll be bound. No warm bed and food such as we have now. No, I'd not change places with any of their kind.'

Kate laughed. 'You have no imagination, Bridget. I'd change places any day.'

She sighed and walked on home, deep in thought. Some evenings later it was Kate who suggested to Bridget that they should go down to the barn again.

'But we have seen the play,' Bridget protested. 'Why go down there again? Ah, I have it, it is the dark young man who ogled you. You have a mind to be admired again, is that it?'

Kate tossed her red-gold hair. 'He can admire me all he wants. I just want to see the players again. Come, Bridget, come with me.'

Bridget shrugged indulgently and the two girls set off down the Cork road. And Bridget prided herself on her shrewd guesswork when she saw the dark youth emerge from the back of the barn during the interval and come forward to speak to Kate.

Bridget shrank back, aware that her own plain face and dun-coloured hair were not the attraction for him. She watched Kate bridle and dimple, toss her head proudly, and finally nod shyly to the youth, who disappeared behind the hay again, apparently well-pleased with himself.

So Bridget was not altogether surprised when Kate spoke hesitantly to her at the end of the play.

'The young actor you saw, Bridie – his name is Valentine – has a mind to escort me home. I told him I was with company, but he was most insistent.'

'Do as you've a mind, girl, what's it to me?' Bridget snapped in reply.

'I would not leave you alone, Bridie, but I'm longing to hear more of their mountebank way of life – where they go, how they live, what famous people they may be asked to perform for. Oh Bridie, would you be very hurt if I go with him?'

'You go. You'll always do what your heart is set on doing, and who am I to stop you. But don't be late, Kate. Be home before the gates are locked.'

And Bridget was gone. She had seen the eager Valentine pressing his way through the throng and did not want to see the disappointment on his handsome face if he found her still there with the lovely Kate.

Bridget sat up half the night in the little garret, waiting for Kate to come home. No doubt she would be all smiles and starry-eyed, happy in the assurance that womanhood was now upon her and men found her attractive. Bridget hovered, heavy-eyed but sleepless, in the little window, watching and ready to go down to unlatch the door. But the hours dragged by and Kate did not return.

When dawn began to creep across the sky Bridget knew she would not come, and with a heavy heart she made ready to explain to the mistress, who would no doubt be very angry.

Mistress Lennie was indeed vexed that her household was thus depleted without warning, and sent a messenger during the morning to the strolling players' barn, to bring back the errant servant. But the messenger returned alone, to say that the players had packed up their hampers and gone overnight. By now they would be over the Dublin hills and away, and Kate with them. Mistress Lennie sighed impatiently.

'Well, there's one mercy,' the exasperated lady said at length. 'The child is an orphan now, so at least I am spared the problem of having to explain to her parents. I wish her well of her wanderings, the wretched child, and I only hope she does not come back a-begging when her gipsy love has had his fill of her.'

And with that she returned to the task of acquiring herself a new kitchen maid, banishing all thoughts of the feckless Kate from her mind.

Barely a mile away, inside the fortress of Dublin Castle, Ormond sat in his chair, no less exasperated than Mistress Lennie. After a lapse of four years since Colonel Blood had dared to try and take him and his castle, Ormond still felt the man pricking him like a stubborn thorn in the foot, although the man himself was never to be found.

Like a mole the fellow disappeared instantly underground whenever he was spotted, only to come up again in the most unlikely places to cause more mischief. For a time there had been peace from the fellow's molestations when it was reported that he was in hiding in Holland, and then when England went to war against Holland there was no more rumour of his movements. It was possible he was still plotting England's overthrow at that distance, for it had been said that he was friendly with the Dutch admiral, De Ruyter, though there was no proof of the rumour.

But then the war had faded into insignificance against the enormity of the plague that had nearly wiped out London, and then the great fire which had only recently occurred and decimated half of London's buildings. Since then there had been signs that Blood was at work again. One report said that he had been seen in Northern Ireland, at Colonel Carr's, and another that he had been seen near Dublin recently and was planning to take Limerick!

And now there was this business of the Covenanters in Scotland. It was almost certain that the dissenting Blood, well-known to have been in correspondence with the Scottish Covenanters, was behind this uprising. But when Government troops penned the Covenanters in amongst the Pentland Hills and killed or captured them all, Blood was not among them. Blast the fellow! He must have escaped in the confusion. The blackguard had the luck of the very devil! Again he had gone to earth.

Where would he emerge and start his trouble next?

In only a few weeks Ormond found out what he wanted to know. Blood was in England, at the home of his wife's family in Lancashire, but was planning to leave and return to Ireland immediately.

'Not if I can prevent it!' Ormond roared, and hearing that Blood was planning to land his ship near Carrickfergus, he sent Lord Dungannon to intercept and arrest Blood there.

But the old fox was too wily. Scenting a trap as he neared Carrickfergus, he ordered the ship to turn about and return to England. Frustrated with rage when he was told, Ormond stamped back into his study and locked himself in to devise another plan.

The Dutch fleet was still hovering about England's shores, but with no intention of making a determined attack for there was every sign of a peace treaty in the air. Unexpectedly word came to Ormond from London that one of Blood's known associates had been captured and was being held in the Tower.

Ormond acted at once. He took pen and paper and wrote to the Secretary of State asking him to transfer the plotter, a Captain John Mason, to York gaol.

'I ask also that you send to accompany him, as if another prisoner, one William Leving, a former conspirator who has now come in to aid the government. He has proved of great assistance to our cause in the past, and will prove an able spy in the present matter.'

Ormond went on to explain to the Secretary that he believed it highly likely that Blood would attempt to rescue Mason, and even if he did not, the four days' journey would give Leving ample time to befriend Mason and extract valuable information from him.

This done, he signed the letter with a flourish, sealed and dispatched it. Then he leaned back in his chair contentedly. Unless he had greatly underestimated Blood's courage and daring, the reckless Colonel would attempt a rescue in person, and then – ah, then!

At the very moment when Ormond sat relishing this thought, two young lovers emerged from a woodland clearing miles away. The young man's arm encircled the girl's slender waist and his head rested lightly on top of her red-gold hair.

'You're so lovely in the moonlight, Kate mavourneen,' he murmured tenderly. 'I swear I love you best of all by moonlight.'

'And will you always love me, Val?' She looked up at him, a teasing light in her green-gold eyes.

'For ever and a day, my beloved. But will you always love me?'

'I will. Oh Val, I will indeed.'

They walked on a few paces. 'Yet you know,' the youth added, 'when Charles says you have learnt enough and allows you to go on stage, you will have many admirers.'

'So I will,' she admitted. She had proof enough of her attractions now. Val's was not the only eye that had watched her approvingly.

'Gentlemen among them, mayhap, who will bring you gifts and flattery.'

'Is that so?' He saw her eyes grow round at the prospect. 'But you'll not be minding that now, will you Val? You'll be proud of me then.'

'Aye, that's true. If only I can be sure of you.'

She laughed at his fears. 'I vow I'll follow you to the ends of the earth, my lord,' she teased, dipping him a graceful curtsey. 'There now, will you be satisfied?'

He took her roughly in his arms. 'I swear you're the most beautiful, tantalising creature I ever clapped eyes on, Kate, and some day soon I'll make you my wife, so none but I can claim you,' he murmured into the thick folds of her hair.

'We shall see,' she murmured in reply, but his mouth stifled any further remarks.

Another hour passed in pleasant dalliance before their footsteps led them back to the barn where the company had made camp for the night. The manager was pacing up and down outside the barn door, his face scowling and sullen in the moonlight.

'Where the devil have you been, Valentine?' he demanded gruffly. 'The magistrates have ordered us to move on at once, and everyone has been busy re-packing but you.'

'Move on? Why?'

'They say they have suffered enough already in the way of stolen chickens from vagabonds the likes of us, and we're not welcome here. But as always when there's work to be done, you're not to be found, off gallivanting with your doxy here.'

Kate rounded on him, her eyes flashing. 'I am no man's doxy, sir,' she snapped, her voice icily polite. 'I am a lady, and will thank you to remember it.'

'A lady, is it?' The manager's eyebrows rose sharply. 'You can act the part well enough, it is true, but a lady i' faith? I doubt it. However, there may be a part for you as a lady in the next play if you mind your manners.'

Val looked crestfallen. The manager turned to him. 'And you'd best be thinking of a good excuse, my friend, for Alida has been raging like a she-cat, stamping around and demanding of everyone whether they have seen you. No one had the courage to tell her you'd gone off with Kate again.'

The young man's dark eyes flashed angrily. 'Why does she spy on me so? She has no claim over me.'

The older man shrugged. 'It has been said for many years that you and she would wed – your parents all hoped for the match.'

'I care naught for what others may plan,' Val retorted. 'I have a mind of my own and I do not include Alida in my plans.' He glanced at Kate out of the corner of his eyes. 'A dark Spanish wench is not to my liking anyway,' he smouldered. 'I like a maid to be fair skinned and golden and biddable. Alida has too fiery a temper for me.'

'Aye, as you'll no doubt find again when

she discovers you!' the manager laughed. 'Go now and help load the wagon, you idle creature, or you'll be no favourite with the rest of the company either.'

Val turned sharply and left Kate standing, hands on hips, near the barn door. The manager eyed her up and down critically.

'Biddable, eh?' he muttered to himself. 'Humph!' and he strode inside the barn to make sure it was cleared.

THREE

It was a hot, still August day in 1667 when Captain John Mason stepped out from the Tower of London, heavily manacled and guarded. He blinked hard in the unaccustomed brilliance of the sunlight, so vastly different from the gloom of the chill, dark cell he had been living in for the past few weeks.

'You are to be sent to York for the Assizes,' the Keeper of the Tower had told him, 'out of reach of your Non-Conformist accomplices in London.' But there was a gleam of hope in Mason's heart, for he was sure that

Blood and Lockyer and Butler, his fellow ringleaders, would make some kind of attempt to free him once they learnt he was out of the dreaded Tower.

He was led across the courtyard and handed over to an officer leading a small group of men. Seven in all, Mason counted. Not too many for Blood and the others to cope with.

'Corporal Darcy.' The officer who had led him from his cell addressed the young man in charge of the troop. 'Here is your prisoner. Take him as you have been directed and guard him well. Remember also to collect the other prisoner from Newgate whom you are to conduct to York.'

The young officer saluted and accompanied Mason stiffly to the coach which stood waiting with drawn curtains at the Tower gate. Mason climbed in with some difficulty, for his limbs were stiff after weeks of disuse. Two troopers climbed in after him, and the others, he presumed from the clatter of hoofbeats, were to accompany the coach on horseback.

The coach trundled heavily across London's cobbled streets for some time, then stopped and waited. After some minutes the door opened and another prisoner, manacled like himself, was pushed unceremoniously into the darkened interior of the coach. He was short and red-haired, his freckled skin pale and his eyes squinting from the bright light. He too had evidently been imprisoned for some time.

He did not speak. He simply grunted, a sound which could be taken for a greeting or a curse, as he fell into the seat opposite Mason. The coachman could be heard whipping up the horses again, and the coach began to lumber off along the London streets.

No one spoke in the coach as the streets were left behind and the coach rolled on over the rutted tracks leading out into the country. Mason saw that the other prisoner was watching him with a sullen, suspicious look, but neither man spoke.

After a time the guards grew bored sitting facing each other in the dark coach, and began to talk. Evidently they thought their chained prisoners harmless enough, and ignored them while they chatted of duty and pleasure, of which inns served good ale and which provided the best wenches.

Gradually it darkened into evening and the guards began to doze, each trying to keep awake in turn. It could not be long now till they stopped for the night, Mason thought, and he was on the point of commenting so to his fellow-prisoner when the other man suddenly spoke first.

'You for York gaol too?'

'I am.'

'What's your name?'

'Mason. And yours?'

'Leving.'

The name signified nothing to Mason. He was obviously not one of their own gang or its collaborators elsewhere, or he would have heard of Leving. He must be for trial for some other kind of felony. Mason turned his thoughts to Blood instead. Would the gallant Irish colonel attempt a rescue?

The coach drew up sharply on the cobblestones of what must be an inn yard. The guards leapt to life instantly, and the prisoners were escorted through the dark yard into the warmth and brightness of a cheerful little inn. Blood would not make an attempt tonight anyway, Mason decided. It would be on the open road, if at all.

The second and third days of the journey up to Yorkshire passed uneventfully, save for the heat and the flies and the uncomfortable bumping and jolting of the coach. Leving had become more talkative while the guards slept, but Mason was not interested in his chat and endless questions. He was straining his ears and waiting and hoping for Blood to appear, and each evening he felt disappointed that the big, black-haired Irish giant had not sprung from the bushes.

It was now the fourth and last day of the journey. The heat in the coach was foetid and Mason's head ached. Leving, to his relief, begged the guards to draw back the curtains and open the windows a little.

'For the love of God, we must have some air in here,' the man gasped, clutching his head as though he too had a severe headache.

One of the guards grunted, looked at the other, and then drew back the curtains on one side of the coach and opened the window. The gush of cool air that swept in was indeed a blessed relief and Mason felt his throbbing head begin to clear.

It was late in the afternoon. Mason felt dispirited. If Blood had been going to act, he'd have moved before now, he felt sure. He would just have to resign himself to a further period of confinement in a filthy, stinking prison. He sighed audibly.

Voices drifted through the open window of the coach. Mason sat up expectantly, hope rising in his heart. Corporal Darcy had reined in his horse to talk to another traveller on horseback. The coach drew up alongside them.

'For York?' the corporal asked.

'I am, but it's so lonely on these moorland roads, I'd much prefer to travel in company with you, officer, if you would permit me.'

Mason leaned forward. He could not see the man's face nor hear his voice distinctly. Could it possibly be Blood or one of the others in disguise?

'Your name and trade, sir?' the corporal questioned the man.

'My name is Scott, a barber, citizen of York, returning from the funeral of a cousin. Please let me ride with you.'

The young corporal, apparently affected by the pleading in the barber's voice, let him fall in behind the coach with the troopers. As the barber turned about and came close by the coach window, Mason saw to his dismay that he was not one of the gang. His hopes had been raised in vain, Blood was not going to attempt a rescue after all.

Mason leaned back on the upholstered seat, all hope now having receded. Leving was looking at him curiously. Perhaps he had seen the look of hope brighten on Mason's face.

'Expecting friends, were you?' he asked gruffly.

'Mayhap.'

'Who, for example?'

Mason shrugged. 'Who knows? One can always hope, even for the impossible and unlikely.'

Leving grunted and lost interest in him. Mason watched the fields roll by, the sun sparkling on the streams and the birds wheeling low. No sign of a town in sight, hardly a cottage even to be seen. It was already late evening; it could not be many miles now to York.

The coach jerked and jolted its way off the main track and down a narrow lane. The going was even bumpier and more un-comfortable than before. Suddenly a cry rang out from one of the troopers behind the coach.

'Horsemen, corporal, behind us!'

The rattle of hoofbeats told the occupants of the coach that the horsemen were in a hurry, galloping swiftly towards them. The seated guards leapt up, opened the door and jumped out. Leving smiled at Mason.

'Your friends at last?' he enquired.

Mason's heart leapt. Could it be Blood, making a last-minute bid? He craned his head out of the window, and ducked in quickly again as pistol shots rang out. Leving's smile faded. He sprang to his feet and peered out.

'Four horsemen with pistols! Two of the guards are wounded,' he said in an incredulous voice. 'The corporal is going to fire back!'

At his words more pistol shots shattered the peaceful countryside. Mason heard stifled cries from wounded men, and elbowed Leving out of the way to look. The corporal, sword in hand, was leading his still unhurt men into a fight at close quarters with the intruders.

Mason could not see the faces of the attackers for they were masked, but there was no doubting the big, burly figure of Blood. The colonel was cutting and thrusting fiercely at the young corporal, and twice Mason saw the blade of his sword, glinting in the evening sunlight, piece and rip the young officer's flesh.

Then another shot rang out and the corporal's horse suddenly crumpled underneath him. Mason heard Leving behind him, his quick gasp of dismay, and then the further door of the coach opened. When he turned to look, Leving was gone, leaving the door of the coach swinging idly behind him.

The open doorway was suddenly filled by the figure of a big, black-haired man. He signalled urgently to Mason.

'Come John, quickly, there is little time,' Blood's voice came from behind the mask. 'Here is a horse – mount and follow us instantly.'

Mason did as he was told in silence and unquestioningly. With a leader as gallant and shrewd as Blood one did not need to question, but simply obey. As he galloped away after Blood and the others he saw men lying in pools of blood, some dead and some near to death, but all of them, so far as he could glimpse, were troopers.

Much later, in the comparative safety of an inn miles away, Mason, Butler, Lockyer and Blood sat talking of the evening's exploit. Blood was in high good humour at having reclaimed his able lieutenant, and drank and joked heartily as they sat by the fire.

'He was a gallant little corporal, sure enough, but he met his match today,' Blood remarked. 'At least three of his troopers were wounded unto death, I am sure, and are doubtless laid out by now. One was already dead, I know it – no trooper, but a man dressed as a traveller, I think.'

'Scott, the barber,' Mason breathed. 'He said he was a traveller. Was he not known to you, then? Not one of the gang?'

'Not he!' Blood roared. 'A traveller, was he? A pity he had to meet his death then, and he as innocent as a babe.' After a pause Blood added, 'But what of the other prisoner I saw slip from the coach in the fighting? Who was he? If he'd had wit enough to stand fast we'd have taken him clean away as we did you. He has likely been recaptured by now.'

'His name was Leving, but I knew him not,' Mason said. Instantly Blood's expression changed. His jaw dropped, his eyes grew fiery, and then he banged his tankard on the table with a gesture of anger. Lockyer and Butler's tankards paused halfway to their lips.

'Leving! Of course! I thought he looked familiar.'

'You know him?' It was Mason's turn to look aghast.

Blood scowled. 'He was once one of us but went over to the government, spying on us and sending word secretly to them. It was some time before we discovered, but he had gone. We could never get at him to silence him. The Secretary of State found him too useful to let him go, and they guard him well.'

Blood rubbed his chin thoughtfully. 'Now why would they be sending him to York with you, I wonder?'

'For trial, I understood.'

'No, not that.' The colonel began to rub his large nose, his brow creased in perplexity. 'It was no mere accident of fate, of that I am sure. There was some purpose in the design.'

Mason interrupted. 'To question me about what I knew, that was it, I am certain. I did not realise it at the time, but now I remember how he quizzed me, casually as it seemed, but now I see how cunning he was.'

Blood's gaze was piercing. 'Questioned you? To what end, John?'

'To discover your future plans, mayhap, colonel, but I did not admit any knowledge of you.'

Blood studied the hearth. 'No, I think they anticipated that we would attempt to free you,' he said at length, slowly. 'And they put Leving there to identify us. He knows me and Butler and Lockyer well. And we, poor fools, have let him escape to tell the tale.'

His thoughtful look darkened to one of anger. 'I scent Ormond behind this strategy, damme if I don't. It is he who has planned this to snare me, I know it is. But by God, I'll be even with him! I have an old score to settle with that scoundrel, after what he did to my sister's husband and to our other colleagues in Dublin. This is just one more of his sins to be accounted for.'

Mason looked puzzled. 'But Leving – if he identifies you, you're done for.'

'Not unless they can catch us,' Blood chuckled. 'It is more likely we shall catch Leving first and silence his tongue. I must send a messenger to find out what became of him.'

Suddenly Blood grimaced. He rolled up the sleeve of his coat and inspected his arm, and Mason saw that there was blood trickling from a gash.

'You're hurt, colonel!' Butler exclaimed.

''Tis naught; a scratch,' Blood demurred. Lockyer hastened to examine the wound and found there was a deep gash several inches long in his forearm.

'Well, thank God it is not my sword arm,' the colonel joked, but his face was pale and the wound was severe enough for him to allow himself to be persuaded to have it dressed and retire early that night.

Within a couple of days word came to Blood's ears that Leving had astonished the wounded Corporal Darcy by coming out of hiding as soon as the fighting was over and surrendering himself again into their hands. They had continued then on their way to York gaol and handed over their prisoner to the governor.

The prisoner, it seemed, had been most loquacious, giving the governor a full account of the attack and the names of the attackers – Thomas Blood, Timothy Butler and Captain Lockyer. He was then thrown back into his cell to await trial.

Blood snorted. 'Await trial be damned! They're keeping him safe from our clutches, that's why he's kept locked and guarded! They want sworn evidence against me at the trial, recorded and irrefutable. But by God, I swear they'll never have it!'

Butler and Lockyer sat silent. Mason watched their leader proudly. He was like an angry god, unpropitiated by the sacrifices offered to him, this great, shrewd, courageous man. But how would he cope with this problem, and silence a heavily-guarded man? He put the question to Blood.

'I know not yet,' the colonel answered broodily, pacing the floor of the inn and having to lower his head to avoid the low rafters. 'Give me time and I shall think of a way.'

He paced the floor for some time, lost in thought and nursing his wounded arm with the other hand. Then suddenly he stopped. He dismissed Butler and Lockyer but signalled Mason to stay.

'I shall write a letter. I wish you to see it is delivered safely to the Lord Lieutenant of Yorkshire,' he said.

'Buckingham?' Mason said in surprise.

'Aye, the Duke of Buckingham himself. I have his ear from time to time and I think he may be of no small help to me in this matter. His hatred of Ormond is well known.'

Blood called for paper and ink and sat down to write, flourishing the quill in the air before he dipped it into the ink and began to scrawl. When he had done and sealed and addressed it, he handed it over to Mason.

'Do not let yourself be seen, but make sure it reaches my lord as quickly as you may,' he said with a hint of a smile.

As Mason gripped the door handle he heard Blood chuckling behind him. 'I'll teach my Lord Ormond a lesson,' the big man laughed softly. 'He'll find he cannot snare an old fox like me so easily.'

The weeks passed. Blood and his companions lay low, sneaking furtively about the countryside, and the government was unable to lay hands on them. Blood had deliberately exaggerated the extent of his wounds and put the story about that he was mortally wounded, so the military's attempts to find him were of necessity half-hearted if the man was dying anyway.

One day in another country inn, Mason and Butler found Blood in dancing good humour as he sat down to breakfast.

'Heard the news?' he demanded jovially, his dark eyes sparkling with pleasure. 'Leving has been found dead in his cell in York gaol. Most mysterious circumstances. No one had access to the fellow, yet he was found poisoned. Most strange, most mystifying, wouldn't you say?'

He crammed a chunk of cold roast beef into his mouth, chewing and smacking his lips with obvious relish. 'So, my Lord Ormond, you must wait a little longer yet before you and I settle our reckoning,' he murmured almost inaudibly around the beef shreds.

51

FOUR

For this latest escapade in rescuing Mason, Blood, Butler and Lockyer were again declared outlaws and a price of one hundred pounds set on each of their heads. But because the rumour was still rife that Blood had been severely, if not fatally, wounded, little serious attempt was made to discover him. So it was with not too much difficulty that Blood and his colleagues were able to disappear completely. For safety's sake, however, the group of plotters disbanded, and each went his own way.

'What will you do, John?' Blood asked Mason as they were parting.

'Oh, I've always had a fancy to play mine host in an inn. I think I'll go to London and set myself up in a tavern there. And you, colonel?'

Blood glanced down at his wounded arm, now fully healed. 'I've put potions and poultices on this damn thing so long I feel I can account myself a physician now,' he joked. 'After all, my potions worked a cure, which is more than I can say of many an apothecary I've met. Aye, I think I'll play the physician in some little town in the country where no one has ever heard of Blood or the Dissenters.'

And so they parted. Blood eventually settled in Rochford, Surrey, calling himself, now, Dr Ayliffe. He sent for Thomas Hunt, who had been an apothecary's assistant, to help him in the work, assisting and dispensing. For the next two or three years life was peaceful and uneventful for the erstwhile firebrand, even if the peace was not to last.

But for Kate Varney, actress with a company of strolling players putting on their fanciful performances in barns and villages up and down the length of Ireland, life was far from uneventful. Kate's promise as a budding beauty at the age of thirteen had ripened into lush fullness that caught and fascinated the eye of every man who looked at her, and well the pretty wench knew it.

Her firm, rounded body and full, pouting lips, her arrogant air and fiery tresses were the means of procuring many a meal when she would have starved else, and more than once the company manager had Kate to thank for softening the anger of a village magistrate who would otherwise have arrested some member of the troupe on a petty charge. Chickens and vegetables were plundered wholesale from market stalls and cows let loose from their fields after surreptitious milking, and somehow the strolling players always escaped the consequences of their lawless actions while the pretty, pert Kate was there to speak for them.

For over the past three years Kate had learnt the extent of her powers of persuasion, and there were no longer any doubts in her mind about her power over men. Valentine had long ago ceased to be her only admirer, though he was still her strongest.

'You have some evil powers, I doubt not, that have him so entranced,' the dark beauty Alida would say savagely, 'else he would have forgotten you long ago. You tease every man who comes your way. Valentine must know you for the fickle jade you are.'

And it was not only Alida who resented Val's adoration of Kate. Charles, the manager, had a pretty, golden-haired daughter named Constance who followed Val everywhere, openly worshipping him with her huge, blue eyes, but he seemed not to notice her. But Constance did not show her dislike of Kate so openly as Alida did. She simply hung her fair head sorrowfully and wept for Val's thwarted love, and hoped secretly that one day he would come to her for comfort.

Charles was unaware of the turmoil in his nest. So far as he could see, his company was thriving, with two lively beauties in Kate and Alida to choose from for his leading lady, and his dutiful daughter always there to play a supporting role. Val was a competent hero, with the dark, good looks that were certain to bring in all the local village lasses, so he was content.

And more than content when Alida, who had eluded his grasp for years, finally became his mistress. He could not understand his sudden good fortune, at his age too, greying and fattening as he was, that such a fiery beauty should so unexpectedly give herself into his arms. But Charles was not a man to worry himself unduly about the motives of actors – they were all a highly volatile, unpredictable lot. Before long, Alida's reasons became clear.

'Charles, darling,' she would say, as she lay in his arms, 'who is to play the queen in the next play?'

'Oh, you or Kate, of course,' Charles replied lazily.

'Why Kate? It is a role perfectly suited to me, Charles, and you know it. I can give the part the fire, the spirit it deserves.'

'So can Kate. You and she are a match when it comes to spitting fire and brimstone, my love, but why concern yourself with next week's play now?'

'Because I want to play the queen.'

'And so you shall if you wish it, my beloved.'

Before many weeks had passed Alida was using her new-found power to press her ambition further.

'Do we need Kate, my darling? Why don't you dismiss her?' she murmured to Charles as they lay together in the hay in the barn.

Charles sat up. He was beginning to understand the drift of her intentions and felt disturbed. Was it simply jealousy of Kate as an actress that Alida felt? Or was it more than that? He was about to put the question to her, to ask her if she was jealous of Valentine's adoration of Kate, when he thought better of it. Why spoil a delectable evening in the hay?

He lay back again, the question unspoken.

'Well?' Alida demanded.

56

'We shall see.'

'When?'

'Soon. After the end of the week when this play closes and we move on.'

'You promise?' Alida's voice was like honey.

'I shall think of it then, not now my beauty. Come, the others will return soon. We are wasting time.'

He drew her down in the hay and she was silent.

When Kate returned with Valentine from the village she sensed the air of triumph about the glowing Alida. She had been uneasy ever since she had become aware of the new state of affairs in the company. Alida had Charles dancing to her little finger now, and it was obvious to all but a fool that she must have taken him for her lover, or how else would she secure the leading role in every play?

Kate did not like the new atmosphere she sensed. Alida was too cocksure, too triumphant for safety. Had she persuaded Charles to take another step to secure her rival's downfall? For the first time she could remember since her parents died, Kate felt insecure. For a long time now it had been she who had called the tune, but now Alida seemed to have ousted her and become mistress of the situation.

Suppose Alida had Charles dismiss her, what then? Where could she go, with no living relatives or friends? What work could she do for a living? To return to being a kitchen maid was unthinkable, after the freedom of the road with the players. No, she must think of some way of outdoing Alida.

To usurp Alida's position as Charles' mistress was possible, but unlikely. Charles was revelling in Alida's attentions. Val then? No, to be his mistress would delight him but achieve her nothing, for he had no more say than herself in the management of the company.

To marry Val then, what of that? Yes, that was a likely plan, for Charles prized Val highly as the hero of all his plays, and he could hardly dismiss his leading man's wife without losing his hero. Moreover, the plan had the attraction of spiting Alida further, for Kate was positive that it was Val she really wanted, not Charles. Constance would be sorrowful too, for she obviously worshipped him, but why should Kate bother her head over that little goosebrain? If the wench wanted him, why the devil hadn't she done aught about it before now?

Yes, marriage to Val would solve the problem. Kate made up her mind to wed him as he had been begging for so long, before the week was out. He at least would be overjoyed when he learnt.

But she was not prepared for the baffled look in his eyes. 'You will marry me after all?' he said in astonishment when in answer to his thousandth proposal, she agreed.

'Indeed I will,' Kate said firmly. 'Why not?'

'Oh Kate, beloved,' he murmured, almost in a swoon with ecstasy. 'I truly believed you never would.'

'Then it is high time you learned not to try and predict what I will do or say,' Kate replied, 'for I hardly know myself.'

Val broke the news joyfully to the rest of the company. Charles clapped his hands in genuinely pleased surprise.

'I am delighted, my boy, truly delighted,' he said, beaming at the company. Behind him Alida stood silent, but Kate could see the fury glittering in her black eyes. I was right, thought Kate, she did plan to get rid of me and is wild with anger now that I have not only bettered her but stolen Val as well.

Kate could not resist the surge of vengeful pride that rose inside her. That would teach the brazen bitch to try to defeat Kate Varney!

So the wedding was planned for the end of the week. On the day before, a band of gipsies came to camp in the neighbouring field, and many of the actresses were anxious to meet them, to see if, perchance, there was one among them who had the gift of foresight and who would foretell the future for them.

'Tomorrow, tomorrow,' Charles said, waving his arms in emphasis, 'not tonight when we have a play to perform. When the wedding is over and we have our own festivities here, we shall ask the gipsies to come then.'

There was, as it transpired, a woman among the gipsies who had the gift, so the gipsies swore. She was their aged leader, their wizened, toothless queen. True, her blank, far-away look indicated that her eyes could see what mere mortals could not, and by the time Val and Kate returned from the church, the actresses were already chattering excitedly in anticipation of her predictions. Only Alida stood aloof, clinging possessively to Charles' arm.

Around the fire, the merrymakers squatted, gipsies and actors alike, tossing back their ale and singing folksongs and gipsy airs. Kate felt content. She had to admit she was not half so enthusiastic about their wedding as Val was, but she was content enough. And tonight, dressed in her wedding gown, the finest jade green silk the company's hampers could bestow, and a sham pearl coronet entwined in her fiery hair, she felt like a queen surrounded by her courtiers.

Alida's silver and white gown, the one she wore last week to play the empress, showed off her dramatic dark beauty to advantage, and well she knew it. She stood with regal hauteur, surveying the frolics, but when Val came forward to kneel at Kate's side and sing a love song to her as he strummed his guitar, Kate saw her cool look darken to one of vicious jealousy. She let go of Charles' arm and came forward to join them by the fire.

At that moment one of the gipsies led out the old woman, the fortune-teller, and the old beldame hobbled up to Alida.

'You the bride?' she croaked in a feeble voice. 'May Providence shine on you and shower you with her blessings, my dear,' she purred, but Alida began to laugh harshly.

'Not me, you old harridan,' she shrilled,

shaking off the old woman's hand from her arm. 'That is the bride.'

She indicated Kate. The old woman turned with difficulty and peered at her in the firelight, screwing up her eyes, then gasped.

'You the bride – dressed in green?' she said incredulously.

Kate's hand fell involuntarily on to the rich green folds of her skirt. 'Yes, why not?' she asked.

The old woman's pale blue eyes were wide, and she shook her head sadly. 'Green is an unlucky colour for a wedding, my dear. No success will come to your marriage from it.'

'Green is the colour of the Irish!' Kate retorted. 'Why should it bring us harm?'

'Please yourself, girlie, but it betokens naught but ill at a wedding. Someone should have warned you. Here, let me look in your palm and see what may be written there.'

Kate offered her hand gladly, in the hope that the old creature would read better news there. The old woman sat down jerkily on a felled tree trunk and held the hand close up to her eyes. Val's expression as he watched the scene was one of deep concern. Kate glanced at Alida. She was smiling broadly and glancing coyly up at Charles.

''Tis strange, passing strange,' the old crone murmured.

'Tell me what you see,' Kate demanded eagerly. Val craned forward. Alida paused in her teasing to listen.

'I see fire – and water. Deep waters. You will cross deep waters.'

'Yes? And what else?'

The old woman pushed Kate's hand away abruptly. ''Tis no good. I see no good for you, child, only trouble.'

'But *tell* me what you see.'

The old creature's bleary eyes looked up at Kate and the whole circle of roisterers round the fire hushed to listen. ''Tis strange, but I see riches – jewels.'

'There,' said Kate triumphantly, turning to smile at Val. 'Riches, we shall prosper after all.'

'No,' the old gipsy woman interrupted sharply, 'Not him. You will be close to fine jewels, but not yours. Especially I see a bloodstone. A bloodstone – that signifies courage, you know. A big, dark man of courage, who will have a great part to play in your life. But before all this there is danger – fire, water, and death. I do not like what I see. I shall return to my bed.'

The other actresses began to protest, for they had not had their fortunes told, but the old woman was adamant. 'I have foreseen enough, I will do no more,' she croaked, jabbing her stick firmly into the ground as she hobbled away.

Val put his arm about Kate's waist. 'Take no notice of the old fool, beloved,' he murmured in her ear. 'We shall be happy, I know it. Come, let us leave others to their merrymaking and away to bed.'

Alida seemed not to notice or to care that they were leaving, but Kate had not missed the look of malicious delight on her face as she heard the gipsy woman's baneful predictions for Kate.

She lay close to Val's hard warmth and felt his protective arms about her. At least now she would be safe from the threat of dismissal. Bloodstone, the gipsy had said. Bloodstone for courage. Strange, but the combination of the words somehow conjured up in Kate's mind a vision of a tall, strong, black-haired man, and his face was gentle despite its unhandsomeness.

'What are you thinking of, my beloved?' Val's voice whispered close to her ear in the darkness.

'Naught. Only the gipsy's words.'

'Put them out of your mind, my angel, for she spoke only the meanderings of a demented old woman.'

'I will, I will.'

Val was silent for a moment, then his lips brushed her ear again. 'Think only of the tall, dark man she spoke of who would change your life.'

'It was of him I was thinking, Val,' Kate admitted, but she did not add that the words had given her a sudden glimpse of the man who had saved her life many years ago. Colonel Blood – the man of courage.

'I am that man, am I not, my Kate?'

'You are, Val, you are indeed,' Kate answered, cradling closer to him. But she knew that this was her first lie to him. Though it was Val's arms which enclosed her as she lay there in the darkness, her mind was full of the daring Colonel Blood.

Outside the barn the merrymakers laughed and caroused and the gipsy music flooded the air with passion and excitement. Only in Kate's heart was there no passion, no exultation, save the tingling caused by the memory of Blood.

FIVE

The autumn of 1670 was drawing in, the leaves had all fallen and the first icy chill of winter was creeping over London. James Butler, Duke of Ormond, buried his ageing bones deeper in his fur wrap and called for the servants to throw more logs on the fire.

He was glad to be back in London again, for the peat bogs of Ireland were no place for a man whose limbs were growing old and rheumaticky. And Clarendon, now in exile, had known what he was about when he built this mansion, for Clarendon House, where Ormond now resided, had enormous fireplaces better able to heat the vast chambers than ever Dublin Castle could be heated.

Once the fire had been refuelled Ormond turned again to the letter in his lap. It was in the King's own hand and dealt at length with the forthcoming visit to England of the young Prince William of Holland. The nineteen-year-old youth was to pay his first visit to England, to pay his respects to his uncle the King, and to James, Duke of York, the King's brother. It was officially to be a visit purely for pleasure, Charles said in the letter, but there were private matters to be discussed between the young prince and the Cabal, political matters which were not to be allowed to reach the public ear. No doubt concerned with the projected marriage between the prince and young Mary, the Duke of York's daughter, Ormond mused.

So it was ostensibly to be five months of festivities, Ormond growled to himself. He knew he would be expected to play his part in entertaining the youth, and after spending many long years in exile with the King when Charles was of a comparable age, he knew how pleasure-seeking and inexhaustible youths of nineteen could be. For this princeling nothing would be too much trouble or expense. It would mean a long, fatiguing round of balls and cockfights, drinking and gaming, horse racing, receptions and dinners.

And now Ormond was no longer Lord Lieutenant of Ireland, but Lord High Steward of England, he would have to take his share in entertaining the royal guest, he knew. So it was with much relief that he learned later that his duties would consist mainly of accompanying the young Prince William to the feast which was to be specially arranged for him by the City Corporation.

The banquet was to be held in the stately Guildhall on a Tuesday afternoon in early December. And it was already November now. Ormond screwed up his eyes and peered out of the window, but still nothing outside was discernible in the thick, brown fog that blanketed London.

He felt vaguely irritated at the prospect of having to leave the warmth of Clarendon House on a December afternoon to face the chilly draughts of Guildhall. It would no doubt be a very lengthy affair, with all the ceremony and pageantry due to the royal visitor. One vast, sumptuous course of the banquet would follow another endlessly, interspersed with tedious speeches of welcome and toasts in fine old wine. It was unavoidable, of course, but once all the official part of the affair was ended, he consoled himself, he could slip away and leave the younger men to continue their festivities as far into the night as they cared. He could return to the comfort and warmth of his mansion and a revivifying bottle of fine old brandy from his cellar.

He called his secretary and began discussing with him the details of the royal visit. When he came to the matter of the Guildhall banquet, his secretary regarded him quizzically.

'What is it, Lacey? Why do you look so puzzled?' Ormond demanded sharply. Usually Lacey was quick, quiet and efficient.

'Do I understand you plan to go to the Guildhall by coach, unguarded, your Lordship?'

'Not at all. I shall travel as I usually do, with my six footmen, the coachman and a runner. What more protection do I need, man?'

The secretary shook his head doubtfully. 'On this occasion it would seem more fitting to include a troop of your soldiers, my Lord. Who knows what malcontents may be abroad? The news of Prince William's visit and what functions he is to attend will certainly become public knowledge, and your old enemies could well make use of this occasion.'

'My old enemies?' Ormond repeated in surprise. 'Every soldier has his enemies, man, and I must have countless. But which of them would attack me?'

'There are those in Ireland who hate you.'

'Ireland is far away, and they are very unlikely to hear of my movements until it is too late.'

'And in England not everyone admires you,' said Lacey daringly, putting his love for his master above his regard for himself. But Ormond was not angered.

'My enemies here are too high born to attempt an assault on my body, Lacey. On my reputation or my position, yes, but on me personally, never. Have no fear. I value your concern for me but I assure you it is unfounded. The worst that may befall me at the Guildhall banquet is a foul attack of indigestion.'

He smiled wryly at his own jest and patted Lacey on the shoulder, then continued dictating his orders. There were so many smaller details to be seen to yet. New clothes, for instance. Ormond would need a new suit or two for the prince's visit. He set about settling this kind of trivia with his secretary, arranging for his tailor to be sent for, measurements to be taken, and fittings. Already Lacey's misgivings had been dismissed from Ormond's mind.

But if the Lord High Steward had known

that not fifty miles away from Clarendon House a country physician was to prick up his ears with interest when he heard of the banquet, perhaps he would not have been so carefree.

The middle-aged Dr Ayliffe was by now accepted by the village folk and respected for his learning, and if the cures he offered them were not always efficacious, well, neither were the panaceas of any doctor, even the King's. No one thought to question his qualification to practise as a doctor, nor asked where he had lived hitherto. Some more observant patients noted the curious soft inflection of his voice, but could not be sure whether it was an Irish or Welsh accent.

But they all noticed his assistant, the handsome young Mr Hunt. He was a striding, lively young man, with gaiety in his voice and a smile in his eye that was calculated to cure the vapours in any of his pretty young patients. In fact, many of the village maidens had been known to go to the doctor's house simply to watch him dispense a concoction which, if only he had known it, was quite unnecessary and only an excuse for the young wench to confide in him and watch his thoughtful nod as he listened.

And so far, young Mr Hunt had seemed to smile on all but favour none. Heads turned as he passed and tongues wagged hopefully, but thus far he had never been seen in a maiden's company – except on his errands of curing. Ah well, the young maidens of the village reasoned, so long as he was not betrothed to anyone, there was yet reason to hope and pray.

But on the outskirts of a little town in Ireland, a young woman lay in the arms of her new young husband and found no joy or achievement in her nuptial state. Val was loving and tender to his bride, but Kate could feel no eager lovingness to repay his ardour.

'Kate, my beloved, are you not happy with me?' he asked her, concern and pleading in his dark eyes.

'To be sure, Val, to be sure,' she murmured consolingly, and could have bitten her tongue for the wicked lie she was speaking. He was kind, it was true, and she liked him well. But love him? This could not be love. Where was the ecstasy, the leaping joy and sweeping peace of love fulfilled that she had always dreamt of? Love of a kind, maybe it was, the tender concern of a mother for her child, but not the fierce, demanding passion between a man and a woman.

But how could she hurt Val by telling him all this? Better by far to respond to his warmth as best she could, and try to reassure him that all was well. She could never tell him that she had agreed to marry him only for safety, to avoid being cast out of the company by the wily Alida.

And Alida's sharp, shrewd eyes missed nothing. Kate found her one day crouching over the fire and whispering to Constance as she added kindling to the flames. Both girls looked up, startled, as Kate's skirts swept in front of them.

'We were just speaking of you,' Alida said mischievously, rising and brushing the flecks of dust from her skirts. 'We were commenting how sad a figure poor Val cuts for a new husband. Such a pathetic face! It would seem his mate does not satisfy the wants of a hot-blooded young man such as he.'

Constance rose quickly from her knees, her face pink with confusion. 'No indeed, Kate, that is not what we said,' she muttered with embarrassment. 'We only said that Val looked a little – dejected.'

'And there are some who would console him if Kate cannot,' Alida added maliciously. 'Are there not, Constance?'

Constance's face reddened even more. 'I must see to my costume,' she murmured, turning away. 'There is a tear in my skirt.'

There was an amused smile on Alida's face as she watched Constance hasten away. Kate was angered by her sneering insolence.

'If not Constance, then mayhap you would wish to cheer Valentine,' she said tauntingly, planting her hands on her hips, 'if only he would look at you.'

Alida shrugged and smoothed her hands down over her hips. 'Why should I care to concern myself with a servant when I can have the master?' she answered coolly. Her glance was amused and supercilious. Kate longed to scratch her fingernails down that taunting, insolent face, to mar her perfect beauty for ever. But she intertwined her fingers tightly behind her back to prevent herself.

Alida continued to watch her mockingly. 'It seems to me you had best make sure of your man before you lose him to another more able to please him,' she said purringly. 'Make sure you are with child soon, or you are lost.'

Kate gasped. Not only was the creature's insolence insufferable, but the very prospect of having a child had not occurred to Kate! Of course, she saw it now. If she grew fat and ponderous, Alida would lose her rival for the heroine's roles in each play. Constance presented no threat to her, for she was too pale and gentle to play a lively, dominating part, and the other actresses were as yet too untrained. And by the time Kate had been put out of action by several months of bulky plodding, Alida's supremacy would be established.

But Alida herself could find that she was with child any day, for by now it was no secret that she was Charles' mistress. What then? Kate could not resist voicing the delicious thought.

'And you, Alida, have you a charm to protect you from conceiving a child? Some magic potion, perchance, from the gipsies?'

For a moment she saw the confidence waver in Alida's eyes, then the dark girl drew herself up haughtily.

'You had best be about your business, madam, or the manager will be asking why your chores are not done,' she snapped icily.

'And you, I presume, are relieved of all chores by virtue of your position as the manager's doxy,' Kate replied calmly. Alida's eyes flashed dangerously.

'I am no doxy, so take a care to your idle tongue, mistress, or you will cut yourself. I am Charles' betrothed.'

Kate gurgled as she threw back her head and laughed uproariously. 'If wishes were horses...' she cried. 'I shall tell Val of your hopes.'

'Do that!' Alida snapped. 'You shall see. In the meantime, watch you do not lose your own husband, mistress, for there are others who wait and scheme, I warn you.'

Kate crossed her arms and eyed her coolly. 'Constance, mayhap, poor child? She presents me no threat. Nor you, Mistress Alida, for I have heard Val say that he would not have you if you were the last woman left to lay in Christendom, so stuff that in your gullet and chew it!'

Kate was aware of the murderous gleam in Alida's eyes as she turned and left her standing by the fire, but the laughter inside her left no room for concern over that jealous creature. Alida only envied what she could not obtain. She loved Val no more than Kate did. Her pride was piqued that he preferred Kate's golden charms to her ill-favoured darkness. Her hatred of Kate was obvious to all, but that she would ever translate her feelings into actions was the furthest thought from Kate's mind.

So that night as Kate lay wide awake, listening far into the night to Val's gentle snoring, she was surprised to hear footsteps creeping stealthily outside the barn where they lay in the straw. Kate held her breath and listened. The footsteps crept furtively closer, till they paused outside the little window, high above where she lay.

Some poacher, perhaps, looking for a chicken? Or a prowler, seeing what he could steal from the company's hampers? Kate moved silently nearer to Val's sleeping figure, to nudge him awake. He would no doubt rush outside to investigate, if she could whisper to him of what she had heard.

Then Kate paused. Perhaps it was only one of the young actors stealing quietly to a secret assignation with one of the actresses or a local maiden. But as she hesitated, she heard the footsteps crunch again, a crackling sound, and then a fiery light appeared suddenly at the high window and arched down to the straw beneath.

Instantly the barn leapt into life, illuminated with a light as bright as day. The straw was ablaze. Someone had thrown in a torch to set the place afire!

SIX

Kate crouched alongside Val's sleeping figure, numbed with shock and disbelief. Who could possibly want to do such malicious harm? But the shock soon dissipated under the glare of the leaping flames and the hissing crackle of the straw. She shook Val's shoulder roughly and pulled him until his eyes opened.

'Val, for God's sake, Val!'

'What is it?' he murmured sleepily, then as the smoke crept into his nostrils he blinked and sat upright. 'Dear God!' he cried in alarm, and, leaping to his feet, he flung his blanket over Kate's head and began dragging her towards the door. Kate felt his arms, strong and protective, curl about her shoulders, and felt too the fierce heat of the flames as he pushed and stumbled, then let go of her to open the barn door.

Once outside, Kate threw off the blanket. She was unhurt, but Val's face was blackened with smoke. He closed the door quickly, then leaned against it, panting, and drawing in lungfuls of clear night air. Then he straightened.

'Wake the others – I'll fetch water,' he cried, and disappeared. Kate did as she was told and soon the night was alive with scurrying figures rushing back and forth to the barn, now a crackling mass of flames. Charles appeared in his nightshirt and organised a chain of men to pass buckets of water, but as the nearest stream was some distance away, the fire had gained an insuperable hold on the barn before water could be fetched.

Alida and Constance watched from a distance, and they too, like Kate, were wide-eyed with horror. Kate could see no sign of guilt on Alida's face, nor chagrin that Val and herself had escaped, but she was convinced nonetheless that it was Alida's hand which had flung the torch into the barn. There was no doubt the wench was a superb actress.

'Are you hurt? No? What a mercy you wakened in time,' she said to Kate in a tone that indicated deep concern. 'And Val too – is he safe?'

Not a flicker in those dark eyes betrayed her as Kate told her that he was, but Constance heaved a deep sigh of relief.

Charles bustled up to them, his face and nightshirt begrimed with soot. Beneath the streaks his face was pale and his eyes bloodshot.

'How is it, Charles, my dear?' Alida asked him in the most tender of wifely voices. 'There was no one else sleeping in the barn, was there? Kate and Val are both safe.'

'They are safe, but I fear the farmer will wreak his vengeance on us for destroying his barn. God knows how we can ever hope to pay for the damage,' Charles groaned. 'We are ruined, Alida, and we shall be lucky to escape prison for this.'

Alida's eyes widened now, Kate saw. This was one consequence of her actions she had not foreseen. Constance gasped and pressed her hand to her mouth. At that moment Val came rushing from the fire, now dying down at last.

'Charles, Charles!' he cried chokingly, 'are there any of our company missing?'

'Why no,' Charles replied, 'I checked that all were safe. Why?'

'Then there must have been a vagabond or a pedlar sleeping at the far end of the barn that we knew naught of, for we have just found him,' Val replied in a faint, far-away voice. He sounded unbelieving, defeated.

Premonition gripped Kate.

'What pedlar? Where is he?' she demanded.

'He is dead. We found him in the barn – dead.'

Silence enveloped the group. Voices cried out still around the barn, but for a moment in the circle no-one spoke. They were thinking the same thought as herself, Kate thought. How were they to explain away a fire and a dead body too?

It was Charles who found his voice first. 'We must fly,' he said, and there was terror in his voice. 'It will mean not only prison, but death for us all if we are taken.'

'No, no, not when we say we did not know he was there,' Alida protested.

'But who is to believe us; strolling players? No, I tell you, we must pack and fly as soon as we can,' Charles went on hurriedly. 'The farmer may have been told of the fire by now, if he has not seen the flames for himself. Gather the others and tell them to get ready.'

Kate hesitated and looked at Val. He was standing listening sheepishly, and at Charles' words he turned to go. It was no use looking to him for a lead, Kate thought, and was about to argue with Charles that they should stay, when a youth came running towards them. He stopped before them, panting and gasping.

'The farmer – he has been woken and told of the news. He is coming swiftly, and is like to burst a blood vessel in his fury.'

'Then we must hasten,' said Charles, taking hold of Alida's hand to go.

'Wait – there is more,' said the youth, clutching his arm, 'he said his nephew was sleeping the night in the barn, and if any harm were to befall him, he would see us all hanged, drawn and quartered before he would sleep in peace again.'

Charles' widened eyes met Val's and then Kate's. All their looks reflected the same thought and fear. Kate's intention to argue with Charles died away instantly. She was shivering violently, even with the blanket wrapped about her shoulders. It was a cold night, misty and frosty as only November could be, but it was not entirely the cold that caused her to shudder.

Charles pulled himself together. 'Go, collect only what is valuable and get to the wagons at once,' he ordered quietly. 'We must fly Ireland tonight, or our heads will be separated from our bodies for sure.'

He grabbed Alida roughly and disappeared. Kate stood gazing at the embers of the barn, her mind in a turmoil. Val took her arm and dragged her away.

Before the farmer could arrive the whole company had climbed into the wagons and trundled off as quickly and quietly as they could into the night. Val's face was set and impassionate. Kate clung to his arm.

'Where can we go now, Val? We are criminals and will be hunted down. Where can we go?'

'To England, I heard Charles say. There we shall be safe and can start life anew. Have no fear, Kate, we shall prosper yet.' He smiled down at her. 'Your gipsy's predictions of jewels and riches will come true yet, Kate. Remember what she said, about fire and crossing water? She spoke truth, I see it now, for we shall take the packet boat to England and then the remainder of her prophecy will come to pass.'

He settled himself down in a rug to sleep on the wagon floor, but Kate could not sleep. She sat upright, the blanket wrapped tightly about her shoulders, as the wagon trundled on through the darkness. She was thinking of the dark man who would alter her life, and the bloodstone. Was the dark man the farmer's nephew who had met his death in the barn tonight? And did the bloodstone signify, not courage as the old crone had said, but blood and death?

Kate felt guilt-ridden. She was responsible for the young man's death as surely as if she had killed him herself. Had she not taunted Alida, telling her that Val would never look at her, until the malicious creature, riddled with envy and full of hate, had been inspired to fling that torch into the barn? If she had not tortured the wench so, it would never have happened.

The dark man would affect her life. Well, so he had if his accidental death forced her to flee to England. This could be the true interpretation of the gipsy's words. Ah well, it was destiny, Kate thought. If it was predetermined so, then it must be. But the thought did not wipe the guilt from her mind.

The weeks slipped by. In England few people noticed the arrival of a band of Irish itinerant, strolling players, for there were many more important and exciting matters to read of and discuss. The visit of the young Dutch prince, for example, and heated debate as to whether his visit was purely for pleasure, as it was said, or whether he was really seeking the hand of the Duke of York's daughter, Mary. It was possible. The King, despite his six years of marriage, had as yet produced no heir although he had a number of illegitimate children, and it could be that the Government were seeking to establish a continuity of the line of Protestant kings by marrying off the Catholic duke's daughter to the Protestant Dutch prince. And this matter of the royal succession was a cause dear to everyone's heart, if the King was not going to succeed in breeding a son from that seemingly barren Portuguese Queen of his, Catherine.

Nowhere in the country, however, was young Prince William's visit more eagerly discussed than at the house of Dr Ayliffe in Rochford. Not so much because the doctor cared about the succession, as that the State visit included a banquet at the Guildhall where the Duke of Ormond was to be the prince's companion.

'At last,' murmured Blood to young Hunt. 'At last the old fox will leave his lair and we shall have the opportunity to reach him.'

'He will be well guarded, Colonel, you can be sure of that,' Hunt replied. 'It will not be easy.'

'Probably so. But naught that is worth while is ever easy, and I have waited a long time. Ormond has yet to pay the debt he owes me for my brother-in-law's life, and many of my friends. It will be a challenge, and a happy one at that, to reach him and exact my revenge,' Blood murmured contentedly.

'But it is seven years since Leckie's death,' Hunt pointed out. 'Do you still carry revenge in your heart?'

'I do. I swore to my sister then that I should never rest until Ormond was made to pay, and now at last my chance has come. Until now I have had to content myself with stirring up trouble for him among the Dissenters, but now – ah, now!'

Blood's dark eyes gleamed in anticipation. Hunt threw himself into a chair and put his long legs up on the table.

'Well, what is the plan? And who is to be in the plot with us this time? Halliwell, Jones, Moore, Simons?'

'Myself and you, Tom, and two others I shall choose. It was a pity you were taken prisoner last summer, for your face will be known now, but I want you there with me.'

Hunt laughed. 'They could not hold me. There were none to bring evidence against me, so who could prove that I was ever a highwayman?'

Blood smiled. 'It was well for us you were, for our doctoring brings us little enough to live on. But to our plan. The Duke always travels in his coach with a guard of six men, as well as the coachman and a runner. I doubt he will change his arrangement on this occasion.'

'And you consider four of us sufficient against them?'

'We shall be armed – and we have the advantage of surprise. If we waylay the coach in a dark street, far enough from the Guildhall and before he reaches Clarendon House, it will be easy enough.'

Hunt eyed the older man thoughtfully. 'And Ormond – are we to kill or capture him? Death or ransom?'

Blood's face hardened. 'Neither – on the instant. I want him captured alive. I shall tell you my plan in detail when I have the other two with us.'

For the next day Blood was busy in his study, writing and despatching letters with instructions of great urgency to the messenger. Then he sat and chewed his nails until the replies arrived. He smiled with gratification when he had done reading, and called to Hunt.

'We make ready to leave for London at

once,' he told him. 'Halliwell and Moore will meet us at the Bull Tavern.'

But then another messenger arrived, and Blood was closeted with him in his study a full half-hour. Hunt was puzzled. The arrangements were complete now, so what was the reason for this earnest discussion?

He had not long to wait to discover. Blood emerged from his study and sent the messenger on his way. Then he turned to Hunt with a triumphant smile.

'Well, my boy, we have the sanction of the high and mighty on our newest venture. Who could wish for more?'

Hunt looked puzzled. 'Sanction? To a kidnapping, Colonel?'

'Aye, lad, the Duke of Buckingham himself.'

Blood was obviously pleased to see the stunned reaction on Hunt's face.

'Buckingham?'

It was incredible. That a minister of the King's Cabal should condone a murderous attack on one of the most powerful men in the government was breathtaking, but then Hunt remembered the rivalry between the two dukes. Blood seemed to read his thoughts.

'Aye, Buckingham hates Ormond, and he

sees me as a means to rid him of his hated rival.'

'But why you, Colonel? He must have scores of men at his disposal willing to play the hired assassin.'

'Because he knows my hatred of Ormond is equal to his own. And also I am in his debt for sundry minor considerations, and he knew I would be glad to oblige him. This way I may secure further concessions from Buckingham.'

'Do I take it then that it was Buckingham who suggested this attack to you?' Hunt was still mystified.

'Not at all,' Blood replied genially. 'The attack was my own idea entirely. It was pure coincidence that Buckingham has sent word to me that he wishes me to devise some way of ridding him of Ormond. He will be overjoyed to learn how quickly his wishes were fulfilled.'

Blood rubbed his hands together happily. 'I think perchance we can count on securing a better lodging house for ourselves soon, Tom, Buckingham is usually generous when he is grateful. Well, what are you staring at?'

Hunt sat forward. 'I am puzzled, Colonel. I never thought you acted for the government, and yet here you are, prepared to work for the Duke of Buckingham. Are you the Duke's man?'

Blood stood erect, drawing himself up to his full height, and glared at the younger man. 'I am the servant of no man, government or rebel. I am my own man, Tom Hunt, and I act as I see fit.'

He turned away sharply and began buckling on his sword belt. Hunt rose and picked up his own. He fingered the blade of the sword to make sure it was sharp, and ran his fingers over the letters T.H. engraved on the hilt.

'Are you ready?' Blood demanded. 'The banquet is the day after tomorrow and I am anxious to reach the Bull before nightfall and make sure Halliwell and Moore know the details of the plan by heart well before we begin.'

'I am ready,' said Hunt. As they reached the door it suddenly flew open and the maidservant stood there. She bobbed a curtsey to the Colonel.

'Excuse me, doctor, but there's Mistress Baker downstairs, asking for Mr Hunt.'

'Mr Hunt, is it?' There was a gleam of amusement in Blood's eye. Mistress Baker was seventeen and a very pretty wench.

'Aye, sir. She would fain speak with him

because she swears the last nostrum he made for her is the only one that has ever been able to cure her headache. And she vows she is dying of the most frightful megrim now, and must see the young doctor instantly.'

Blood grinned good-humouredly. 'Then I swear the wench must die of her headache – or the heartache – for she can have none of the young doctor now.' He threw back his head and laughed loudly. 'But no – tell Mistress Baker that I regret both Dr Hunt and I are called away instantly to visit a friend up north. We shall be away at least a week.'

The maid bobbed again and withdrew. Blood clapped Hunt on the shoulder and laughed again. 'The village wenches will miss you, I fear, Tom.'

Hunt sighed, a deep sigh of relief. 'I shall be grateful for the respite,' he smiled, and the two men went downstairs.

SEVEN

It was bitterly cold even in the depths of the wood. The leafless trees offered no protection at all to the group of players camped in the clearing, and Kate shivered and shrank into her cloak although she was crouched low over the camp fire.

Charles sat on the step of his wagon, his elbow on his knees and his chin resting on his clenched fist, in what he knew to be a classical pose of dejection.

'Alas, my children,' he moaned aloud, adopting towards his company the paternal air that angered Alida. 'Alas, I fear we can find no work in this inhospitable country. No one wishes to venture from his home on a cold night to watch the players perform.'

'Nor is any farmer willing to let us make use of his barn,' Kate pointed out, 'so we have no place to perform nor to sleep.' She shivered again.

It was true. The local villagers and farmers had been even more suspicious than those at home in Ireland. Mayhap it was their

Irish brogue which worried the locals, Kate thought, and they were regarded as no more trustworthy than tinkers and thieves.

Charles sighed deeply. 'We must not lose heart, my children, but remain optimistic ever. It will soon be Yuletide, and with luck we shall be engaged to perform in some rich gentleman's house.'

The idea obviously appealed to Charles, although the others simply cast him desultory looks and went on munching their supper. 'Indeed, yes, that is a good plan and one we must work towards,' Charles went on eagerly, his apathy gone and a fierce enthusiasm causing him to leap up and pace up and down before the fire, his cloak flying negligently from one shoulder and his hair all tumbled awry in this enthusiasm.

'Yes, we must tout for custom,' he cried, pushing a stray lock of hair back out of his eyes. 'We must all go out instead of sitting idle here, and seek a customer wealthy enough to employ us and offer us hospitality for Yuletide.'

He smiled brightly at Kate and then at Alida, who descended from the wagon. Kate knew what was going through his mind. He would send out the wenches to ply for custom, in the hope that a pretty face might soften a hard heart, and if that ruse failed, there were still other advantages to be gained.

She guessed right. Before Kate and the other actresses set out Charles pointed out to them all that just to be within a wealthy house gave opportunity for eating. 'A prosperous farmer will be only too glad to send you to the kitchen for food, and once there, you can snaffle what you can to bring back for the rest of us,' Charles said slyly, and Kate waited for him to say more. But he forebore from suggesting that they offered their services in any other way.

Several of the young girls returned from that first foray with hunks of bread and chicken legs, concealed within the folds of their sleeves, but no one had secured a request for the company to perform at Yuletide.

Charles rubbed his chin thoughtfully as he sat on the wagon step and listened to the wenches' accounts of plentiful food in warm, well-scrubbed kitchens.

'Well, if we are to secure no work to see us provided for,' he murmured as if to himself, 'then we must make shift to do what we can for ourselves. Alida,' he called, and with her help and advice, the girls set to, under

Charles' direction, to sew huge pockets to conceal under their skirts.

'Make the pockets easy to reach, either through the placket or through the waist-band,' he ordered them, 'then whatever you see to steal, be it food or valuables, slip it quickly into your pocket.'

None of the actresses raised an eyebrow in query at his order. Stealing had always been part of their life in the way of an odd chicken or two, and Charles' new order was simply an extension of the old way of living. As he had pointed out to them, times were unusually hard now for them, exiled from their own country under fear of death, unwanted in England, and in danger of perishing in this bitter cold. Dire need authorised extreme measures, and stealing was but a mild offence.

So Kate was not unduly surprised when Charles had the idea of whore-mongering. It was but a small step from suggesting theft to suggesting selling their favours, and judging by the alacrity with which most of the wenches acceded to the idea, it appeared that some had already raced Charles in reaching this conclusion.

One frosty day Kate approached the main door of a large, solid, respectable-looking house and rang the bell. It was a fair size but not affluent nor large enough to entertain a company. Here she must obtain what she could for the moment.

An elderly woman opened the door. 'Yes?' She eyed Kate suspiciously.

'I should like to see your master,' Kate replied.

'The Reverend Amos is busy, but I'll ask if he wants to see you. Your name, mistress?'

'Mistress Varney.'

Kate stood patiently on the doorstep while the housekeeper closed the door again and went to speak to her master. A reverend, she had said. Good. If he practised according to his sermons, he should be prepared to offer some Christian charity at least to his needy brethren.

The door opened again. 'The master bids you enter,' the housekeeper said quietly, and Kate followed her in. The woman led the way down a corridor, her feet pad-padding in soft slippers, and she kept glancing back at Kate curiously.

'Here,' she said, opening a panelled door. Kate went in and heard the door close behind her.

A balding man with pince-nez pored over a book that lay open before him on a desk.

The chamber was sparsely furnished and not at all comfortable, Kate noticed. No rugs lay on the polished floor, no cushions on the high-backed, sombre chairs. Even the fire burned low in the vast grate. Obviously the reverend was a man of self-denial, more concerned with the life to come than with the needs of the present. He glanced up and looked at Kate curiously over the top of his pince-nez.

'Mistress Varney?' he said quietly. 'What can I do for you? I know you are not one of my parishioners. A traveller, mayhap?'

'Aye, sir.' Kate bobbed him a curtsey. 'We are a group of players, sir, passing through your part of the country. Times go hard with us, reverend, for we have no food and no work. Perhaps you could help us, sir. An act of Christian charity, mayhap.'

She smiled gently and watched his puzzled face soften. If she played the niece pirouetting proudly for indulgent uncle, as it were, possibly he would react in a suitably avuncular manner.

He clicked his tongue and shook his head sadly. 'It is mighty cold to be living out of doors, child,' he murmured.

'It is indeed, sir.'

'And I think I detect by your soft voice

that you are no native here. From Ireland, mayhap?'

'Aye, sir.'

'Where the weather is notably more clement than in England. No doubt you are feeling the rigours of our English winter sharply?'

'Indeed, sir.'

He looked very concerned. If she let him prattle on while she stood subdued by his desk, maybe he would produce blankets or a cloak to help shield her from the cruel frost.

After a moment's thought the Reverend Amos rang the bell. 'Mrs Sharp,' he said to the housekeeper when she answered the summons, 'take this child to the kitchen and feed her well. Then when she is warm and fed, bring her back here to me.'

Kate sat on a high stool at the deal kitchen table and ate hungrily of the delicious beef stew the woman heated up and set before her. The housekeeper took little notice of Kate now, busying herself with basting a duck roasting on the spit, and then, satisfied that it was done, setting it on the table to cool. Then she cut slices off a freshly baked loaf, and Kate devoured them quickly, relishing the crisp, nutty flavour.

Mrs Sharp went out of the kitchen while

Kate was still eating. Now was her chance. Instantly the rest of the new loaf disappeared through Kate's waistband, down into the capacious pocket beneath. Hastily opening cupboards and drawers Kate found little else she could conceal in her skirts. Silver cutlery might clank when she was recalled to the parlour and give the game away. No, she must reluctantly leave the silver plate and pewter and concern herself only with food this time.

She prodded the roast duckling gingerly. It was still rather hot. She blew on it, and then had an idea. Making sure there was no sound of Mrs Sharp returning, she opened the yard door and put the duck outside. Within moments it was cool enough to handle. Kate replaced the plate and secured the duckling firmly under her skirts, then sat down again on the high stool and went on munching bread.

Footsteps approached and Mrs Sharp padded in. 'Are you ready? The Reverend will see you now,' she said, and turned again and led the way out. Kate followed, feeling somewhat uncomfortable with a warm, greasy duckling flapping awkwardly against her thighs.

'Come in, child, sit down,' said the

reverend genially. Kate sat on the leather chair that faced him across the desk, and at once her lips pursed up tightly. The reverend was not to know that she was pouting her lips so roundly in a determined effort not to shriek with pain and shock. As she sat, the duckling had tilted against her bare thighs and although its exterior had been cooled by exposure to the yard air, the innards were still scalding hot, and a fiery mixture of grease and stuffing cascaded down the inside of Kate's thighs.

She sat rigid until the pain passed, then gradually relaxed. She had not heard a word of what the Reverend Amos had been saying, but listened to him now.

'So I consider it my duty, as a man of God, to do what I can for you, my child,' he was saying, arching his fingertips together. 'I cannot, unfortunately, act for everyone for there are so many of you in your company, but I can set an example to others by taking you into my care. You are an orphan, are you not?'

Kate nodded dumbly, not trusting herself to speak yet. The reverend smiled contentedly and rose to come round the desk. He pulled up a leather chair so that it was almost touching Kate's knee, and seated himself slowly upon it.

'Ah, yes, a poor, unfortunate, unwanted orphan, one of the world's derelicts. I see it as my duty to care for you myself, to take you under my roof and be a protector to you,' he murmured sadly. 'Poor child, no mother, no father – you did say you had no father, did you not?' His wide blue eyes narrowed with satisfaction as Kate shook her head.

'Do not look upon it entirely as the goodness of my heart,' he went on after a pause, 'for I too would benefit from female company such as yours, mistress. My mother died while I was young. I have no sisters, nor wife, and Mistress Sharp goes home to her cottage when she has seen to my wants.'

Kate looked at him enquiringly. He looked into her eyes and a light gleamed. 'So you would be all to me, child – sister, wife, mother, all.'

His hand rose, hesitated, fluttered, then fell on her knee. Kate drew in her breath sharply, not from any sense of prudery but because of her awareness of the stolen duckling, not many inches away from his hand.

His hand still lay there, as if forgotten, as

he went on talking. Cautiously Kate turned so that his hand fell away from her knee. Still he talked on, raising his hands as if in emphasis and letting one fall idly on her knee again.

This time Kate removed it with her own hand firmly. The clergyman's faraway look became bright. 'How touching, how reassuring to one's faith in humanity,' he commented, patting her again. 'I truly believe you are a maiden of modesty and virtue, despite your years of travelling the roads. How very refreshing, after all one hears of the wanton behaviour and looseness of actresses.'

Kate watched his hand, still patting her knees commendingly, as if mesmerised. One inch further and he would feel the bulk of the duckling. Then to her horror the pale fingers slid towards the opening of her placket.

'Still, methinks you and I could be good friends, could we not, mistress, in return for the food and warmth and clothing I would provide for you as long as you stayed with me?' The unctuous voice flowed as smoothly as the flaccid fingers. They pressed urgently on the bare skin of her knees now, under the blue broadcloth skirt, and slowly but insistently the fingers were gliding upwards.

Kate leapt up, thrusting his hands away so sharply that the clergyman all but lost his balance and he had to reach for the floor to stop himself from falling off his chair. Kate towered above him in simulated anger and outrage.

'How dare you, sir, and you a man of the cloth! I came to you for help and instead you insult me thus! Do you take me for a trollop?'

She stormed towards the door, then paused. 'I am grateful to you for the stew and bread, sir, and now I shall return to my friends.'

She slammed out, past the startled Mrs Sharp and outside into the country lanes where she started to run. Before long she stopped. The clumping bulk of the duckling made running impossible, and the grease which had poured out of it had coagulated into a white, greasy mess on her legs out here in the cold. Kate sat down and scraped the mess off with a handful of grass, laughing till the tears flowed. If only the Reverend Amos had known that her virtue stemmed only from a desire not to be caught with a stolen duck!

Was that the only reason? She questioned herself as she walked back to the camp. Would she be prepared to sell herself for security? Kate's laugh now was mirthless. Of course. She had already done so when she made a loveless marriage with Val for security's sake. Where would the difference lie in being a whore?

And the reverend, was he any more hypocritical than herself, in wanting to satisfy demands of the flesh without love? He was a man, after all, subject to desires just as any other man, whether he wore the cloth or no. No, she and he were alike in their sham appearances. He only acted a part as she had done herself often, on stage and off.

But she could not resist the urge to retail the incident to Charles and Val and the others as they sat eating the duck around the fire that night, her voice rippling with laughter as she told them how she tried to keep the clergyman's preying fingers off the duck. Only Val did not join in the laughter. 'Would you have been so determined to stay his hand but for the duck?' he asked suspiciously. Kate laughed, and repeatedly he demanded to know the answer, his voice growing querulous and testy.

Finally, when they were alone, Val grabbed

Kate by the shoulders. 'Well?' he demanded.

'What would you have me say, Val?' Kate protested.

'The truth, of course.'

'Why then, you must have it, husband. I should do what is best for me.'

'You mean you would sell yourself if necessary?'

Kate shrugged. 'If it should be necessary, there would be no alternative, methinks.'

Val glowered. 'I am your husband and have rights which I will grant to no other. I forbid you to sell your favours, whatever Charles may say.'

Kate glanced up with a smile. 'Yet I have seen you go off into the bushes in the summer with a lady many a time. Do you think me blind? Am I not to have the same freedom to provide for us as you have had in the past?'

She was aware of the fierce anger on his dark face as she swept away from the fire, and also of Constance's pale concern as she watched. She would console Val for his wife's waywardness, Kate felt sure, as she pulled the rug tightly round her and went to sleep.

In his candle-lit bedroom the Reverend Amos made his prayers on the bare floorboards as brief as possible that night, for it was too cold to linger overlong out of bed in a nightshirt.

'Oh, and St Paul, you were right about women,' he added as an afterthought. 'A temptation sent to lure godly men from the path of righteousness. I thank God for delivering me from temptation today.'

He adjusted his nightcap and climbed into bed, congratulating himself on his firm purpose. Already the sting of Kate's slap had faded from the back of his hand, so he was easily able to convince himself that she was the evildoer who had sought to lead him astray.

Thank Heaven he had been able to withstand her onslaught!

EIGHT

The Duke of Ormond leaned back inside his comfortably upholstered coach and yawned unrestrainedly. At last, eight o'clock in the evening, but at last he had managed to slip away from that infernally boring banquet.

The young Prince William had seemed to enjoy it well enough, for he was still there carousing with the other young blades of the court. But after five hours Ormond had had more than his fill of the exquisite food and wine and speechmaking, and was anxious only for the comfort of his bed. By now the rest of his family and most of his servants would be already abed.

Ormond lay back against the head-cushions and dozed as the great coach lumbered slowly along London's streets.

In the Bull Tavern near Charing Cross Colonel Blood sat by the fire with Tom Hunt, Dick Halliwell, Moore and Simons. He called out to the landlord to send them more wine and pipes and tobacco to pass the time, then turned again to his friends.

'It must be growing near the time now, comrades,' he murmured softly so the landlord would not hear. 'Are you sure you know your parts well?'

A murmur of assent met his question. Blood paused while the pot boy poured out more wine, wiped the table and withdrew.

'But what do you plan to do with Ormond when we have him?' Hunt asked. 'I know only that you wish him taken alive, bound and gagged, and mounted behind Simons on horseback. But then whither?'

Blood put down his wineglass and leaned forward. 'I did not wish to reveal too much too soon. I know only too well how easily news leaks abroad about London, and I could take no risk. Now, however, I shall tell you. Ormond is to die.'

'But you stressed so firmly that he must not be harmed,' Simons protested.

Blood raised a hand. 'Indeed I did. He must be alive and well when we escort him to Tyburn, there to hang him like any common felon.'

The other men looked at their leader silently. They knew and respected him too well to express surprise or disapproval. Blood gazed into the fire and smiled.

'Aye, a hanging at Tyburn for the old devil, that's what I've planned this long while. No quick and speedy death by the sword in a struggle as an old soldier would prefer, but a slow, painful death, an ignominious death such as he inflicted on my brother-in-law. He shall know the feel of a rough rope choking his life away. He shall know the shame of death like a petty criminal.'

He jerked himself out of his absorption and looked up quickly. 'We are all prepared then? Pistols loaded, swords sharpened?'

The replies of the others were cut short by the cry of a footman passing outside in the street.

'Make way!' he cried loudly. 'Make way for the Duke of Ormond!' The group around the inn fire looked at each other silently. The huge, burly figure of Simons shifted uneasily. His was the task of carrying Ormond behind him to Tyburn. The footman's calls died away. Blood pushed his still half-full glass away and rose.

'It is time,' he said quietly. 'Come.'

The pot boy came out from the kitchen and watched the men leave the inn, two still smoking their clay pipes. He crossed to the table, saw the glass with wine still in it and picked it up. The innkeeper was not about. Eagerly the boy lifted the glass to his lips and drained it off. Through the inn window he could see the five mounted figures of the men who had just left, drawing away from the inn door and making towards Pall Mall.

Jeremiah, the night porter at Clarendon House, snuggled deeper into his cloak and was glad of the wooden box provided for him at the gate of the mansion. It was very cold and quiet. Most of the family, in the way of all gentlefolk who rose early of a

109

morning, would be drawing their bed-curtains cosily about them and settling down to sleep now, the fortunate creatures.

Jeremiah's envious eyes turned from the dark shape of the house to the huge iron gates. It was after eight o'clock. It could not be long till the homecoming Duke's coachmen shouted for the gates to be unbarred. It was very dark. The moon flitted occasionally into sight from behind a high bank of cloud, but it was wan and pale and gave little light to see by. But for the sputtering torchlight rammed into the iron bracket on the wall, there would have been no light in the court-yard at all.

Footsteps echoing across the courtyard roused Jeremiah as he was about to drowse. Jim Clark, one of the footmen, came into the arc of light from the torch.

'Cold night, Jeremiah,' said Jim, rubbing his hands and blowing on them. Jeremiah was nodding his agreement when the sound he was expecting came to his ears, the noise of a heavy coach rumbling up the street.

'That's His Grace's coach,' he muttered in satisfaction. Years of training made his master's coach instantly recognisable. Jeremiah rose and hurried to unbar the gate. Clark helped him pull them back.

The horses drew the coach inside and stopped. To Jeremiah's amazement no coachman sat on the box, nor was there a footman in sight. To his horror he found the interior of the coach empty too. Jeremiah's jaw sagged and his eyes grew wide. Clark stared at him in alarm. What could have happened? Footsteps came running and stumbling along the street and a white-faced coachman practically fell into the courtyard. Jeremiah seized his arm.

'What's amiss? Where's His Grace?'

The coachman gasped for breath, leaning heavily on Jeremiah's arm. 'Set upon by thieves,' he managed to gasp out at last. 'Seven or eight of them, in St James' Street.'

Clark pulled Jeremiah's arm. 'Come, let's go look for him,' he said.

'Take care,' cried the coachman, 'for they are villains. They overpowered the footman and dragged out the Duke on the ground. The last I saw of him they were pulling him towards Piccadilly, none too gently either, and for aught I know they may have killed him by now.'

Jeremiah and Clark did not wait to listen further. Together they ran off down the street in the direction whence the coach had come.

They reached St James' Street, breathless, and paused. At the place the coachman had mentioned there was no sight of the Duke or his attackers.

'Towards Piccadilly,' muttered Jim. 'Come.'

The two men ran on past Devonshire House and down towards the Knightsbridge road. As they neared the crossroads they heard the sounds of muffled shouts and curses, scuffling and fighting.

'Here they are!' cried Jeremiah. 'Let us at them!'

There were figures sprawled on the ground, two men scrabbling in the mud. One of them, a huge giant of a man, rose suddenly at the sound of Jeremiah's voice, letting go his hold on the other man, and pulled out a pistol.

Another figure appeared from the shadows and both men simultaneously fired their pistols at the shadowy, muddy figure lying in the road. The sudden, staccato report took Jeremiah's breath away. From out of the darkness a third figure appeared.

'Fools!' he cried. 'Come, here are your horses!'

The other two attackers ran to him and took the reins of the horses he led behind him, mounted and sped away into the night.

Lights began to appear in the windows of neighbouring cottages, and night-capped heads peered out into the darkness. Jeremiah and Clark bent over the man in the road, and had difficulty in recognising him, so utterly covered in mud and filth as he was and barely conscious.

'"Tis he,' murmured Jeremiah at last. 'See, here is the Order of the Garter on his chest.'

Clark helped him lift the Duke clear of the mud-filled street and lay him on a cloak on the grass. The Duke was too breathless and beaten about to speak, and Jeremiah was sad. Who would want to harm his old master so?

Finally Clark and he laid the old man on a gate and carried him carefully home to Clarendon House, where a physician, brought in as soon as the coachman had raised the alarm, waited to minister to the Duke.

It was with great relief that Jeremiah heard later that the old Duke was hurt, but not too badly, and some days in bed would soon see him well again. Jeremiah was happy. The Duke had a stern, forbidding manner, but his servants loved him nonetheless.

In another tavern far from Clarendon House that night sat one who did not love the Duke at all. Colonel Blood was in an unusually savage mood.

'What in heaven's name misfired?' he demanded of his companions sharply. 'I saw you had taken Ormond safely and I galloped ahead to see the road to Tyburn was clear and all was ready, and when I returned, I found your horses running loose and then you and he rolling merrily in the mud like boys at play. Explain!'

Simons cleared his throat uneasily. 'It went as we planned, Colonel, up to a point. We bound and gagged the Duke and then the others seated him behind me on my horse and bound him to me as you bade us.'

'What then?' Blood roared.

'We began to ride off after you, Colonel, but the Duke is a big man and a strong one. He fought wildly and managed at length to fall from the horse, dragging me down with him,' Simons explained unhappily.

'Dragged you down? Did I not choose you because of your size and strength, and yet you tell me that Ormond, old man that he is, succeeded in pulling you off your horse? Simons, you are but a whey-faced woman.'

Simons hung his head. Hunt tried to help. 'It was not entirely his fault, Colonel.'

'I care not whose fault it was.' Blood's

voice was low with menace. 'I only know Ormond was in my grasp at last, Tyburn awaiting his villainous neck and you let him escape. That I cannot forgive.'

Hunt called for ale. 'Come now, there are more pressing matters to concern us, Colonel. We may well have been recognised tonight, in which event we may not be free ourselves for long. We must go into hiding.'

Simons and Halliwell muttered agreement. 'Aye, it is no small matter to attack a minister of the King. The government will be outraged and our heads will pay if we linger,' Halliwell said.

Hunt cleared his throat. 'I have mislaid my sword,' he said casually.

'Mislaid it? How so?' Blood demanded.

'I think I left it in the fray.'

'Is it the one with your initials on it?'

'I regret so.'

Blood sighed. 'Then we shall be recognised for sure.'

'Aye,' said Simons, 'but mayhap we have not altogether failed you, Colonel. Halliwell and I both fired shots at the Duke as he lay in the road. It is possible one of us hit and killed him.'

Blood grunted. 'We shall see.'

And indeed they did. From their hiding

place the conspirators heard how shocked and outraged the people of London were. News came to them of the anger at Court, and the government's determination not to rest until the malefactors were brought to justice. They also heard that the Duke, shaken and battered, was soon restored to full health, and Blood growled angrily.

For weeks Blood, Hunt and the other plotters were forced to lie low. No-one came to apprehend them, nor were their names ever mentioned.

'Fancy that now,' commented the innkeeper one day. 'They don't even know who made that dreadful attack on the Duke. I hear as the House of Lords has had to appoint a committee of sixty-nine to investigate into this business. Fancy that, sixty-nine lords.'

And for another month news filtered through to Blood that the committee was hard at work, aided by its secret agents and the testimony of the ale-drawer at the Bull Tavern. They heard also that a sword with the markings T.H. on it had been found in the mud at the scene of the attack.

'Then I at least will be known,' said Hunt.

He was right. At last the Lords' committee drew up a Bill naming Thomas Hunt,

Richard Halliwell and Thomas Ayliffe, and calling upon these men to surrender themselves.

Blood laughed shortly. 'Surrender ourselves? Not yet, my friends, while there is still work to be done.'

So the government waited. Huge rewards were offered for the capture of the attackers, but no culprits were found.

James, Duke of Ormond, at last recovered from his ordeal, sent privately for Justice Morton, the London judge whose name struck terror into the hearts of all highwaymen.

'I know whose hand I detect in this work, Morton,' Ormond said, 'but I cannot prove it. Will you look into the matter discreetly for me? Discover where Blood and Hunt are now and what they do. I know that outlaw Blood is at the bottom of this affair, though the night was too dark for me to see and recognise any of my attackers. See what you can do, that I, in my position, cannot.'

He did not add that he secretly agreed with his son, Lord Ossory, in his opinion that the Duke of Buckingham was Blood's instigator in the deed. Ossory had openly challenged Buckingham in the presence of the King and, receiving no answer, had vowed publicly to avenge himself on Buckingham if his father should ever come to any harm. All London already knew of the incident, and how the King had had to placate the young man.

So Justice Morton went away, but he could discover nothing save that Blood, Hunt and Moore were reputed to be in or about London somewhere. For the third time in his life Blood was declared an outlaw with a price on his head. Arlington, the Secretary of State, whose secret agents had been busy, confided in Ormond that he was sure that Blood and Halliwell, Moore and Simons, were the miscreants but he had no proof and so, reluctantly, he was obliged to let them stay free.

Ormond sighed. As yet more weeks passed and the new year of 1671 came to London, no trace of the attackers yet unearthed, he realised he would not be avenged upon Blood. One day he would see Blood in the Tower for his sins, but it was not to be yet. He would have to be patient a little longer until the colonel grew foolhardy enough to come out into the open and reveal himself for the criminal that he was.

Meanwhile, Blood returned to Surrey with his assistant, Tom Hunt, and began practising again as Dr Ayliffe. He too sighed impatiently and hoped the chance would soon come again to even the score with Ormond. Even without Buckingham's prompting he hated the man enough to want to watch him suffer. Some day he would.

NINE

Yuletide came and passed with but little demand for the strolling players' services, and Charles became more and more dejected. Inside the deserted old mill where the troupe had taken refuge from the winter's icy winds he seated himself on a raised platform and cupped his chin in his hands. His mournful eyes surveyed the rest of the company, most of them lying wrapped tightly in their covers or pacing to and fro to keep warm. Now and again their movements disturbed a sleeping rat, which darted from its hiding place under an empty flour bin and sent a flurry of dust over the sombre scene.

He sighed aloud. The last few weeks of

extreme cold and hunger had depleted their ranks enormously. Of the original company all but fifteen had left to find work elsewhere in taverns and kitchens; anywhere that food and warmth could be found. When the warm spring came again, Charles knew he would be hard put to it to try and cast a play from those remaining. If matters did not improve soon, he would be obliged to dismiss the faithful few who were left, and his beloved company would no longer exist.

It was sad. His gaze roved over those who still followed him. He still had his leading man, Valentine, but the sparkle had gone out of the fellow lately. He was taciturn and sullen. Not surprising really, for ill fortune had depressed them all.

Kate came in from outside, her face flushed with the cold and her eyes sparkling. She was closely followed by Constance, her pretty face framed by the thick hood of her cloak.

Kate stamped her feet. 'It's freezing,' she said, 'and I think it is like to snow soon.'

'Have you brought food?' Alida's voice snapped the question from behind her. Charles turned to look up at her. Her face was set and hard.

'A few vegetables,' Kate replied, producing a handful of root vegetables from under her cloak.

Alida's tongue clicked. 'And you?' she asked Constance. Constance hung her head. 'I see. Then we must be content to starve yet another day,' Alida said icily.

'And what have you to contribute?' Kate retorted.

Charles intervened. 'Come, my beauties, let us not quarrel. Constance, make us a stew of the vegetables, my dear, while we consider what is to be done.'

Constance set to work in silence, her fair hair falling forward, thus screening her face. Charles sat down thoughtfully and Valentine went on whittling away at a piece of wood. Kate took off her cloak and bent to warm her hands over the fire.

Charles stood slowly, put one foot on the platform and raised his hand. 'Listen my friends, the time has come for decision. We can find no work at this time in our legitimate profession, and unless we act quickly we shall starve. It seems to me inevitable, sad but inevitable, that we must part company at last.'

He cast a mournful look at them all as they listened. 'Unless a miracle occurs, I see no other way out of our problem,' he said sadly.

Kate squared her shoulders. 'Nonsense. We have survived thus far, have we not?'

Alida's eyes flashed. 'And what more can we do, pray? Will you have the women become bawds to buy our food? Is that what you would have us stoop to?'

Charles looked away quickly. Kate fancied he had already had this thought in mind himself and had been reluctant to suggest it. Alida was awaiting her answer, a sneer on her full red lips.

'Why not?' Kate replied carelessly. She heard Val's quick intake of breath. Alida stared. Charles' gaze was still averted. 'Well, why not?' Kate went on. 'Of what use is our much-vaunted virtue while we starve? Have we not already stolen and cheated? I cannot see that there is much difference in whoring.'

Alida came forward, her hands on her hips. 'You, it seems then, would be willing to sell your body?' she sneered.

Kate lifted her chin defiantly. 'Aye. And you?'

Alida shrugged and turned away towards Charles. 'I am in a somewhat special position or I would willingly join you,' she

122

said, sliding a hand across Charles' shoulder. He looked up at her, mystified.

'I shall join you.' It was Constance who spoke, to everyone's surprise. Her pale little face was fixed. She looked firmly at Kate. Charles looked startled.

'No, my child, not you,' he said hurriedly.

'Why not?' Alida demanded. 'She is old enough and pretty enough to secure customers for her charms.'

'No.' Val spoke lowly but clearly. 'I have no wish to be kept by your sacrifices, ladies. Nor will I have my wife a common bawd.' He set down the knife and piece of wood he was paring and put his arm about Kate's shoulders. 'I will not permit my wife to act the wanton, and that is the end of the matter.'

He drew Kate firmly away with him. In a far corner of the old mill he sat on a heap of straw and regarded her sadly. Kate, not for the first time, began to feel irritated by his huge, spaniel-like eyes watching her reproachfully. She drew her shawl tightly about her and paced up and down in front of him, reluctant to sit by him. She felt prickled by his virtuous outrage, knowing it to be a sham. He continued to watch her sadly. Eventually she turned on him.

'Why do you feign so?' she spat at him. 'Why do you act still, even off the stage?' He looked at her in surprise. This angered Kate even further.

'Feign? Act? I am not acting,' Val protested mildly. 'I do not want my wife a strumpet on the streets, that is all. Is that so surprising?'

Kate stared at him. 'Since it would not be the first time, neither for me or for you, why protest now when we are starving? Believe me, I am not anxious to play this part, but my belly rumbles with hunger, Val. Why should you presume to stop me now?'

'Not the first time?' Val echoed faintly. Kate's patience snapped. She faced him squarely, hands on hips and feet planted firmly astride.

'No, and well you know it, so do not pretend. Do you take me for a fool? How often did you disappear with a fine lady for the evening and reappear with new hose or a new finger ring, and was I supposed not to have eyes in my head?'

'But you – you said not the first time for you either?' Val's eyes were rounder and sadder than ever. 'I had no notion, truly I did not.'

'You lie! How else do you fancy I could provide for you what you demanded? Last winter, when you swore you could walk not another step till you had a pair of new boots, how do you think I obtained the fine leather ones on your feet now?' Kate stubbed her toe viciously at Val's outstretched foot. His gaze fell to the boots.

'These were a gift from Lord and Lady Darcy, when we performed for them at the castle last winter,' he murmured. 'A tribute to my playing, milord said.'

Kate laughed shortly. 'Aye, a gift from His Lordship, Val, not my Lady. A tribute to my performance, and not on the stage either. Do you remember his ugly red face and stubbly grey beard? Do you fancy I should have humoured him but for your need of boots?'

Kate stood towering over Val's bent figure, her eyes flashing in scorn. He did not look up. As she had guessed, he had known all along how she came by the boots.

'You knew,' she spat at him. 'You knew, and said naught, you weak, spineless fool! You could keep silent so long as it benefited you. You could be kept so long as the words were not spoken!'

She turned away quickly in disgust lest she poured out too venomously how much she despised him now. She walked angrily up and down for a few moments and then came back to face him, her mind made up. His head still hung dejectedly on his chest.

'I have decided. I shall go and seek work like the others,' she said quietly. Val looked up slowly. 'Do not argue. I am determined,' she said, and walked away to join the others at the further end of the mill.

Charles' gloomy face lit up as she approached. Alida watched her defensively.

'Well?' asked Charles, and Kate could detect the note of hope in his voice.

Kate jutted her chin. 'I shall go. We shall all go, we women, shall we not?' The other girls about assented quietly, Constance among them. Only Alida was silent, and Charles appeared not to notice.

'Good, good,' he said eagerly. 'What are your plans?'

'Two or three of us to visit each nearby inn and tavern to seek custom,' Kate replied firmly. 'And there's no time like the present so we must adorn ourselves and begin tonight.'

Val had approached the group quietly as she spoke. He hesitated on the fringe of the knot and listened.

'With luck we shall not reappear tonight,' Kate went on, 'having found ourselves bed and board elsewhere. But we shall return in the morning without fail. Understood?'

The girls in the group nodded. Alida remained silent and unmoving. Kate looked at her queryingly.

'Is it agreed, Alida?'

All eyes turned to the dark beauty. She tossed her head. 'It is as you wish it, Kate, for I have no part in this business.'

Kate fixed her with a strong look. 'It is agreed that all the women undertake this venture. Why should you presume to remain apart?'

Alida's smile was scornful. 'It is as I told you before, Kate Varney. Finding myself in a somewhat special position, I do not feel it incumbent on me to join you.'

'Meaning your special position as mistress to the company manager?' taunted Kate.

'Not at all.' Alida paused and flicked an imaginary crumb from her skirt. She was enjoying her moment and lengthening it to good effect, as a well-trained actress should. 'I find myself in a particularly vulnerable position where harlotry would be ill-advised for me. You see, I am with child.' She held her head proudly erect.

Alida must have been delighted to see the shocked surprise on her audience's face,

Kate thought angrily. She had chosen her moment well to reveal her secret, letting the other women become involved in the scheme and knowing full well she would be spared on account of her condition.

And Charles. Kate looked to see his reaction. He was gazing at Alida wide-eyed with surprise, but already a happy gleam was beginning to flicker. Doubtless he would be a yet more willing slave to Alida from now on.

For a moment the suspicious thought crossed Kate's mind that Alida could be lying so as to avoid the night's foray. Then she remembered how oddly Alida had been behaving lately, even refusing her minute portion of vegetable broth, saying that it made her feel queasy. It was indeed possible she was carrying a child, damn her. Somehow she turned every disadvantage to her advantage.

Kate felt a hand on her elbow and looked round. Val stood close. 'And you, Kate, how do you know you are not with child?' he murmured apologetically. Kate knew it was a feeble attempt on his part to rescue her, but he was too weak to lie outright, boldly and clearly. She wrested her arm away.

'I am not with child, Val, nor am I like to

be,' she said coolly. Inwardly she wished she felt as sure as she sounded. She had no knowledge of any of the wise women's remedies and preventions against conceiving a child. Mayhap this new occupation would prove too hazardous unless she sought help quickly. Too late now, however, to hesitate.

'I am ready to go,' she said firmly, tossing her red-gold hair so that it caught and reflected the glow of the fire. 'Who goes with me?'

Val watched the group of wenches leave, silent and heads erect. He could not help noticing that not only Alida but Constance too was missing from the group, but Charles waved them off and wished them godspeed, and appeared not to notice his daughter's absence.

Kate was the last to leave. Her red head was still held high, her small nose pointing roofwards and her lips taut and unsmiling. Val felt very sad. Somehow he knew that he and Kate were taking different roads now, and he felt deserted and let down.

A tear hovered on his lower lid. Val brushed it away testily. Oh well, come the spring and performances of their best plays again; he would be sought after, nay pursued, by the prettiest wenches in England. Why waste his sadness on a fickle wife?

What a shrew Kate was becoming, to be sure. She had even accused him of condoning her infidelity, of knowing about her and Lord Darcy last winter. To be truthful, he had had his suspicions about the matter, for leather boots were far from cheap, but to say he knew and permitted her behaviour for the sake of new boots, well!

Constance appeared silently at his elbow, her face pale in the firelight, and she sat down quietly beside him.

'Why have you not gone with the others?' Val asked her.

'My father would not allow me,' she replied softly. What a gentle voice the wench had! Not shrill and accusing like Kate's. Now with a maid like Constance, one could relax and forget one's troubles, Val mused, watching her as he sipped the broth. She would never accuse her husband of infamy.

He sighed and leaned forward over the fire to see if there was any more broth left in the pot.

Kate and the other actresses struggled on in the icy winds until they reached the outskirts of the village. Three of the wenches went into the first tavern they reached, and Kate and a young lively girl named Polly walked on to the inn.

As they crossed the cobbled yard an appetising odour of roasting meat drifted out and met their nostrils. Polly sniffed and sighed longingly.

'Oh, any man'd be worth a good meal of that,' she said, her eyes closed in ecstasy.

'Come now, you must take care to drive a hard bargain, child,' said Kate admonishingly. 'To settle for a good meal only will not feed our friends back at the mill. A meal, and a groat or two, that will suffice.'

Kate sounded far more businesslike and confident than she felt. Her knees wavered as she pushed the door of the inn open. Suppose the landlord recognised their intent and had them thrown out? Suppose she acquired a rough, tough customer who would not pay when the time came? How was she to deal with him?

The noisy taproom gushed welcoming warmth about them as they entered. Heads turned to inspect the newcomers curiously, but Kate was unaware of their gaze. The savoury smell of roasting pig was mouth-watering, and she felt almost dizzy with

131

hunger. She led Polly to sit on the high-backed settle, and called for wine.

Polly nudged her in the ribs. 'What shall we use for money, to pay for the wine?' she asked in a whisper. Kate laid her finger on her lips and smiled. Now she had seen the admiring glances of the other customers, the pedlars and tinkers, the merchants and farmers enjoying themselves after a day's work. With luck they would need no money to pay for the wine.

But somehow Kate felt far less confident than she had done back at the mill. Her self-assurance then had been but an act of bravado, and now she was here with possible clients a mere hand's reach away, she felt frightened and unsure. Too late now to back down, however. For the company's sake she must go on.

The landlord brought the wine and looked at the two girls quizzically. Kate smiled broadly at him to allay his fears, and as she put the Canary to her lips she surveyed the long, low raftered chamber and its occupants.

'He looks kindly,' said Polly timidly, indicating a red-faced, laughing youth, a farm worker judging by his grimy smock. Polly's lashes dropped demurely when she saw he was watching her with evident interest.

'He's yours,' laughed Kate, and turned her head slightly to see who sat further back in the shadows of the mullioned window bay.

From the gloom a pair of dark, earnest eyes regarded her intently over the top of a pewter tankard. The eyes were familiar. Where had she seen that dark-eyed, humorous gaze before?

Memory stirred and reached back into the mist. A big, black crow, yes, that was it! Kate's heart leapt and caught in her throat. It was the laughing, teasing look of her childhood hero, the legendary Colonel Blood!

TEN

Kate's hand wavered as she set the Canary wine down again on the table, her fingers shaking so much she was afraid to spill it and draw attention to herself. Polly's quick eye noticed however.

'What is it, Kate? Do you recognise someone?' she asked.

Kate shook her head. The drinker in the bay had also set down his tankard, and despite the gloom she could see he was young and handsome, no more than twenty-two or three, far too young to be the notorious colonel. In any event, the Irish adventurer was probably still lurking deep among the bogs at home for all she knew. It was the dark, humour-filled eyes of the youth that had suddenly evoked a memory of her hero, no more than that, she assured herself.

But still her heart raced on for some minutes. The eyes had been regarding her closely with an air of obvious interest. Polly noticed it too, when she craned about to see what had captured Kate's attention.

'Methinks you and I both have a beau for the evening,' she murmured in Kate's ear, 'but what do we do now?'

'Wait,' said Kate firmly. 'They will take the lead if they are sufficiently interested.'

They did not have to wait long. Presently the red-faced youth approached their table shyly and blushed and stammered furiously as he begged the ladies to grant him and his companions the pleasure of their company at supper.

Polly smiled and dimpled and inclined her

head, then turned to Kate questioningly.

Kate smiled. 'Do you join the gentlemen yonder, Polly, and mayhap I'll join you later. Thank you, sir,' she added to the young farmer, and he proffered his arm to Polly, who took it and let herself be led away.

Kate sat alone, sipping her wine and feeling her stomach turn over with hunger. Mayhap she had been a fool to forgo the chance of a good supper, but she still felt the stranger's eyes on her back and hoped he would come to her.

At last, when she had almost given up hope and was beginning to regret her impulsiveness, a shadow fell across her table. Hope leapt inside her, and she began to look up, then took hold of herself. She continued to sip her wine.

Someone above her head cleared his throat. 'Your pardon, mistress,' a deep voice said.

Kate allowed herself now to look up, and her heart thudded. It was he, the young man with the searching dark eyes from the bay. Now, by the light of the candle, she could see he was indeed young, with a strong, kindly face and finely dressed in a green velvet suit, with elegant lace at the throat and cuffs. She felt suddenly aware of her

135

own shabbiness. Carefully as she had prepared for the evening's outing, no amount of brushing and smoothing could hide the travel-weariness of her once-elegant gown and cloak. Kate blushed.

'Sir?' she murmured elegantly.

The young man bowed slightly. 'Madam, I should be greatly obliged if you would dine with me, as I should much prefer to dine in company rather than alone. I perceive that you are a traveller like myself. Would you allow me to offer you some refreshment?'

Despite the stiffness of his words his tone was friendly and easy. Kate appeared to pause and consider. Inwardly she was longing to plunge a knife into a hunk of that delicious-smelling pork, but outwardly she seemed cool and considering.

At length she waved him to take a seat. 'Be pleased to sit, sir. As you say, to eat in pleasant company is much to be preferred to dining alone.'

The young man smiled broadly and pulled out the stool. 'My name is Thomas Hunt, mistress. May I enquire how you are named?'

'Kate Varney.'

He rubbed his chin thoughtfully. 'You are not long arrived from Ireland, mistress?'

Kate's eyes widened. 'How did you know?'

'Your voice, Mistress Varney, has lost none of the lilting softness of the Irish.'

'You know Ireland, Mr Hunt? Perhaps you too are travelling thence?'

He shook his head. 'I know it a little, but it is some time since I was there. No, it is from London I am travelling, back to my home in Rochford, not far from here.'

He turned and beckoned the landlord, who, having taken his order, bustled back to the kitchen. Kate took advantage of Mr Hunt's preoccupation to study him further. He had gentle creases at the corners of his eyes that betokened a sense of humour, and his lips were full but firm.

She shivered a little. He was a gentleman, not the kind of man she had come thither to seek as a client. He would be too discriminating, too fastidious to dally with her, and even if he did, it would be for him a passing attention to a pretty wench rather than a commercial proposition. No, she could not try to solicit this man as a client. Instead she would simply enjoy his company – and his offer of a meal.

Her mouth watered at the thought, and she hoped she would be able to wield a fork with some measure of restraint when the food was finally set before her. Young Mr Hunt smiled and leaned on his elbows, chatting amiably until the platters arrived.

Kate toyed with her fork in the food delicately, though the impulse to gobble was strong. She sipped her wine and ate languidly, as though flavoursome pork was an everyday occurrence in her life. Thank heaven for her acting ability, she thought.

But her platter was quite clean before she allowed the pot boy to remove it. Her stomach rumbled uncomfortably with the unaccustomed weight of food within it, and Kate had to conceal an unexpected belch in a contrived fit of coughing.

Hunt leapt to his feet and began patting her back. 'Are you choking, Mistress Varney? Landlord – more wine, quickly!' he called, and when Kate had managed to signal to him between coughing and laughter that all was well, he sat down reluctantly again, but this time next to her on the settle, still holding her hand in concern.

Kate did not have to feign the fluttering that pervaded her body, nor the excitement that he caused to ripple through her. She withdrew her hand slowly and he let it go reluctantly.

For some time they sat and talked, and at

last Kate decided she would have to leave. She could attempt to gain no other client while Mr Hunt was near, and there was no other reason for her to stay. Except that she was enjoying his company. Moreover, Polly had by now disappeared with her young admirer. Kate gathered up her gloves and made ready to go, excusing herself with a smile. Hunt looked surprised.

'I cannot allow you to leave yet, mistress!' Kate raised her eyebrows. 'After so nearly choking yourself, madam, I must insist that you stay a little longer yet and rest,' he went on. Kate smiled.

'By what authority do you insist, sir?'

'I am a physician, mistress, and I advise it.'

Kate sat down again in surprise. A physician! She had guessed him to be a gentleman, but a physician! Her friends would be mightily impressed to know she had attracted a gentleman of such worth. He was talking quietly, of the Dutch Prince's visit to London. Kate tried to pay attention to what he was saying.

'And then, I heard, as the Duke of Ormond was on his way home from the banquet his coach was waylaid and attacked. They say the Duke was lucky to escape with his life.'

''Tis more than he deserves,' Kate murmured. She screwed up her gloves angrily. Hunt turned to look at her curiously.

'You know of Ormond?' he asked in surprise. 'Ah, but I forget! You are Irish and have no doubt lived under his rule.'

'His tyranny,' Kate corrected him sharply. 'I have seen the cruelty of his soldiers. I have watched my countrymen suffer and die because of his callous heart. Ah, indeed, Mr Hunt, I know of milord Ormond. He gave rise to the starvation and misery in our country that robbed me of my parents. I have reason to remember him.'

Kate's voice was low, but the bitterness was unmistakable. Suddenly she became aware that Hunt was regarding her questioningly, and there was an air of pleased surprise in his look. Kate threw off her mood and laughed.

'Well, as you see, Mr Hunt, I have no love for milord Ormond, and if some ruffians saw fit to attack him, then they have my approval at least.'

'Hush, mistress, it would do you no good to let your views be known here,' Hunt warned her. 'It would be dangerous for you. But let me add, your views are not far removed from my own, so you have no

140

reason to fear me.'

But Kate was not listening. 'If only my childhood hero was here, he would put paid to milord's account in no uncertain fashion, I am sure,' she mused. 'In fact, I wonder...'

'Wonder what, mistress?'

'Whether I detect the hand of Colonel Blood in this business,' Kate said as if to herself. Instantly she jumped, for Hunt's tankard hit the table with a crash as he lowered his hand suddenly.

'Blood?' he repeated.

'The Colonel has always hated Ormond as many of us did, and many's the time I hear he has been a thorn in milord's side,' Kate said. 'I wonder if he had aught to do with this matter?'

'Indeed it has been rumoured so,' Hunt admitted guardedly. 'Blood's name was on many lips in London when the Duke's mishap was announced.'

'There! I knew it!' Kate declared with satisfaction. 'He was my hero many years ago when he rescued me as a child, and I see now that my faith in him was not misplaced.'

'He rescued you?' Hunt echoed in surprise. 'Tell me, mistress, how it came about.'

So Kate told the handsome young man, whose head bent close to hers in eager interest, of the attack on Dublin Castle and of the little girl who wept for a doll's lost arm. Hunt listened intently while she told of the big, black-haired man who carried her off from under the horses' feet and revealed at last who he was.

Hunt nodded. 'That sounds indeed like Blood's impetuous nature,' he commented. 'Only he would be diverted at the height of a campaign to notice the plight of a child and act upon it.'

'You know Colonel Blood?' It was Kate's turn to sound surprised, but Mr Hunt spoke of her hero as if he actually knew him.

'I have met him.' Hunt's reply was guarded.

'Often? Where and when?' Kate leaned forward in her eagerness, and Hunt smiled.

'It was some time ago now, mistress, but it is widely rumoured that he is an impulsive fellow, given to unexpected actions. No one truly understands the fellow, not even his friends, I believe, for he keeps his counsel well and no-one but he knows all that goes on in his head. A veritable enigma, our friend Blood.'

Hunt laughed suddenly, a low, gentle laugh as if to break the atmosphere of reverie and veneration he had implied by his words, and snapped his fingers for the pot boy. Kate realised that the hour was late and the customers had almost all disappeared from the taproom while she had been engrossed in conversation with this handsome young doctor.

'No, no more wine, I thank you, it is late and I must continue on my way,' she said, rising and fastening her cloak.

Hunt rose also, his dark head a clear foot above her own. 'Then if you will allow me, Mistress Varney, I will escort you home. A moment, if you please, while I see about ordering a coach.'

'There is no need,' said Kate in alarm. 'I have not far to go. A coach is quite unnecessary, I assure you.'

'Then I shall walk with you, mistress, for the roads at night are unsafe for a lady.'

He returned to the bay to collect his cloak, hat and gloves, then spoke quietly to the landlord. He came back then and took Kate's arm with a quiet, proprietary air that brooked no refusal, and led her outside.

The air was cold as they crossed the cobbles of the inn yard and Kate gathered her cloak tightly about her. She was troubled how to elude Mr Hunt, pleasant though he was, before she reached the rutted lane leading down to the old mill, and would have to explain where she was staying.

The moon flitted from behind the clouds every now and again and by its light she could see his crisp, dark hair curling about his brow and his serious, thoughtful face.

'Which way?' he asked as they came to the road.

'The rectory, near the bridge. But please, do not accompany me all the way,' Kate replied. She hoped he would believe her to be staying at the rectory, and that she would prefer him not to be seen in her company.

He nodded and walked on, still holding her arm tightly since the road was rutted and uneven. It was pleasant to feel his warm strength, so reassuring and protective, a feeling she never had while with Val.

As they neared the bridge, Kate slowed her steps and finally stopped. She turned and looked up at Hunt.

'I thank you for your concern, sir, and for your pleasant company, but there is no need to go further.'

Hunt's face smiled down at her in the moonlight. 'I have enjoyed our meeting immensely, Mistress Varney, and hope I shall have the good fortune to meet you again ere long. Do you stay long in the neighbourhood?'

Kate hesitated. She would dearly like to meet again the handsome young doctor who evidently shared her admiration for the gallant Colonel Blood, but how could she? He took her for a lady, while the company of actors were waiting patiently for her to bring back her whore's earnings to keep them alive. And if she earned nothing, how long would the troupe remain in this country village? Any day now Charles might disband the company or move them on.

She looked again at Hunt's expectant face, and felt a rush of excitement. She must see him again! Dammit, she would see him!

'I think I shall remain here a few days longer,' she murmured, feeling her cheeks grow hot with embarrassment. She was glad her hood shaded her face from his view.

'Then do me the honour to meet me again tomorrow evening at the Pheasant and dine with me,' Hunt answered quickly. 'I shall look forward to our meeting. Eight o'clock?'

Kate nodded dumbly, too happy to speak. Suddenly she felt Hunt grasp her hand and looked up at him in surprise.

'Here, take this,' he muttered, pressing something into her palm and folding her fingers over it. Kate opened her hand wonderingly, and by the moonlight she saw a gold coin nestling in her palm.

'What is this?' she asked, her eyes wide.

Hunt averted his head. 'I cannot let you return empty-handed,' he murmured.

'I do not understand you, sir.'

'You came in search of money, I know. You granted me your gracious company all the evening, and for this I am in your debt. That you did not earn money as you intended is my fault, but I do not wish you to suffer, that is all.'

Kate felt the blood rush to her cheeks. He had guessed her mission to the Pheasant, and she was filled with shame. But her shame hid behind a façade of anger.

'Sir! You mistake me! How could you believe it?' She held the coin out to him in an angry gesture of refusal. 'Take your money! I will have none of it when you malign me so!'

His face was furrowed, whether with displeasure or perplexity she could not tell. He shook his head slowly.

'No, keep it, mistress. I guessed you to be one of the troupe of Irish vagrants everyone knows to be staying hereabouts, and I saw your friend in the inn leaving with her young squire. I think my guess is not far from the truth and I cannot have you return to your friends empty-handed. Take it. Let them think what you will. I shall be awaiting you at the Pheasant tomorrow night.'

Kate's anger was genuine now. Fury raced through her veins. It did not matter that he had guessed aright, but she was livid that he took her for a common bawd yet he had appeared to treat her as a lady until now. He had been teasing her, toying with her for an evening's diversion.

Tears blinded her eyes, and half-choking with rage, Kate turned from him and stumbled away down the path leading to the mill. Damn him for his superior, taunting manner. She never wanted to see him again.

ELEVEN

The moon had glided behind a high bank of cloud and the old mill was in utter darkness when Kate reached the foot of the lane. Not a light glimmered. She groped her way round the shadowed side of the mill till she felt the door latch beneath her hand, turned it softly, and went in.

The only sounds to be heard were the snores of sleepers and the soft scuffling of rats as she crossed quietly to the far corner where she and Val slept. The rest of the troupe were abed early. She wondered if Polly had returned and told them aught of what had passed in the Pheasant.

Without undressing Kate snuggled down beside Val in her wrap and lay there wondering if he were awake and was simply ignoring her. She knew he had not wanted her to go tonight but he was not a man decisive enough to prevent her. No doubt he would simply sulk.

Finally, Val never having stirred or spoken, she fell asleep. She was awakened at dawn by Polly who was shaking her shoulder vigorously.

'Look!' said Polly triumphantly, holding out a coin. 'My farmer friend had money enough! How did you fare, Kate? Your friend seemed very finely-dressed, a gentleman to be sure.'

Kate sat up, rubbing her eyes. Val lay still on his back, but his eyes were open wide, watching.

'Well?' demanded Polly, 'did you earn aught?'

'Aye,' said Kate slowly, and from her bodice she drew forth the gold coin Hunt had given her. She saw the veiled look that crossed Val's face, and he turned away.

'Well done,' said Charles, who had come up behind them. 'A good night's work, the pair of you. Now, with what the others brought too, we shall not starve for the next week at least. Polly, you go down to the village with Constance and bring us bread and ale and cheese and some meat for breakfast. I' faith, it will be wonderful to eat a hearty meal again!'

He went off, rubbing his hands with satisfaction, and Polly disappeared to find Constance. Val lay with his hands behind his head watching Kate as she rose and pulled her shawl over her shoulders. She waited for him to speak. Surely he would ask her questions, or reproach her.

His lips remained sullen and silent. It would be only reproaches and recriminations when he did open his mouth, Kate decided, so she did not speak. After a while he rose and left in silence. Later she saw him deep in conversation with Constance. No doubt he was showing Kate he preferred Constance's virtue and submissiveness to her own behaviour. Ah, well, Kate shrugged.

She could not concern herself deeply with Val's childishness. If she gave him time he would break his sullen silence.

It was evening before he spoke, and when he did he was full of smouldering outrage. He sat before the camp fire, chafing his hands together and spreading them to the glow.

'Well, what manner of customer did you find for yourself last night?' he demanded sharply.

Kate turned to him, but he kept his set face averted. 'A gentleman, Val, but he was not my customer. He was kind and gave me money only because he enjoyed my company.'

Val snorted. 'You expect me to believe that?'

Kate shrugged. 'It is true. You may believe what you will.' Val turned and looked up at her. 'And in any event,' Kate went on, 'you should be glad however I earned the money. You should be glad that I care enough about you.'

'About me? You went to earn a whore's fee for the whole company's sake, not for me. If you are speaking the truth, you were lucky to escape.' He gazed into the flames for a few moments, brooding moodily, then spoke again without looking at her. 'But you shall not go again. As your husband I forbid you.' The words spat out, low but clear.

Kate stared at him. 'You forbid me?' she echoed in astonishment.

'You heard me aright, wife. You shall do as I bid you,' Val said, hugging his knees morosely.

Kate was speechless for a moment. Why, she wondered. Was it possible Val was speaking out of love and concern for her?

'Tell me why?' she said in a low voice.

Val looked up, and she could see the dull glow in his eyes. 'Because I do not wish it. Because Charles can keep his mistress and daughter out of whoring and I do not see why he should be able to do so if I cannot. Let Polly and whoever will, go play the strumpet, but not my wife. You will tell Charles you will not go again, and that is final.'

Val turned away from her. Kate seethed. She was furious. He spoke, not from love but from wounded pride. That was typical of him! If he had shown concern, protectiveness, she might have considered his request, but vanity! Kate raged inwardly. She would not be dictated to by such a cowardly, vain creature! But rather than let the impetuous words spill out, Kate turned sharply away and left Val crouching over the fire.

It was only when she sat hunched with her arms about her knees on the barn floor that Kate remembered the lean, dark Thomas Hunt and her promise to meet him again at the Pheasant tonight. She dearly wanted to see the kindly young doctor again, and made up her mind to go to the inn whatever Val might say.

As dusk fell she brushed and bound up her hair and prepared to leave. Val eyed her with a frown.

'Where are you going?' he demanded.

'To the inn,' Kate replied, continuing to bind her tresses.

'I have told you you shall not,' Val retorted angrily, taking her arm. Kate shook it off.

'I have a mind to do as I please,' she said quietly. 'And as I am going, not for whoring, but only to see a friend, there is no harm.'

'I have forbidden you to leave here.'

'I heard you.' Kate stood up and drew on her cloak.

'You defy me?' Val's voice was hoarse and sharp. Kate did not answer him. The next thing she knew, a stinging slap made her face tingle and redden. She put her hand to her cheek in wonder, and Val stood glaring at her, his face dark with fury.

Kate stood erect. 'I shall do as I have a mind,' she said again, and turned to go, but Val caught her arm and swung her about to face him.

'If you leave now, you are no wife to me,' he snarled angrily. 'I shall disown you.'

'As you please,' Kate replied smoothly. She did not feel as unconcerned as she sounded, but she was not going to let Val win. Thus far in his life he had won all he desired through his vanity and petulance, but not any more. Inwardly she rebelled angrily and vowed to do as she pleased.

Val let her arm drop. 'Go, then,' he growled, 'but have a care. I shall seek comfort in other arms if you desert me.'

Kate parried his threat. 'Do then, I shall not mind.'

She saw Val consciously change his role. He passed a limp hand across his brow and closed his eyes. 'I am not well,' he said wearily, 'I am sickening for the ague, and yet you would leave me thus. How thoughtless and selfish you are, Kate.'

She eyed him thoughtfully. He did indeed look flushed, but that was anger, not illness, she was sure. 'Bid Constance make you a syllabub, then, and get you to bed early. I shall not disturb you when I return,' she said quietly, and as she walked to the barn door and out into the night she was aware of Val's surprised look as he watched her go. He had fully expected his feigned illness to detain her, but she was not to be cozened thus easily by his deceit.

Thomas Blood sat back in his highbacked chair and watched young Hunt prepare to leave. The young man seemed to be grooming himself with somewhat more than usual care this evening, and Blood was curious.

'What is it to be tonight then, Tom?' he asked. 'I think you have some special venture in mind, so much care you are taking over your appearance. Has one of our local wenches found her way to your heart at last?'

Hunt turned and smiled leisurely. 'It is indeed a maid, Colonel, but not a local wench. It is a beauty I met yesterday while riding home from London, a veritable flame of beauty, and I am to ride to meet her again at the Pheasant.'

Blood sat up with interest. It was not often Hunt was smitten. More often he was hard put to it to elude the grasp of predatory wenches, so this one must be specially enticing. 'Tell me more, Tom. Who is she?'

Hunt turned from the mirror, satisfied that his neckband was now as it should be, and Blood could see his eyes were shining. 'She is the most bewitching creature I ever beheld, with hair like fire and the deepest green eyes I ever saw. Oh, Colonel, if you could only see her!'

Blood rubbed his long nose and mused. She was obviously not one of the local maidens for he had come across them all in the past twelve-month. 'A traveller, mayhap, or a visitor?' he enquired.

Hunt laughed shortly. 'One could say she was a visitor, Colonel, but she is not the lady you undoubtedly expect. She is a strolling player.'

Blood sat upright. 'A player?'

'Do not be scornful, sir. She is a beauty, I swear.'

'I am not scornful, but interested.'

'So you would be if you met her, for she is a compatriot of yours and, moreover, an ardent admirer.'

'Indeed?' Blood's bushy eyebrows arched.

'It seems you saved her once, when she was but a child, when you attempted to storm Dublin Castle. She lay in the path of the troopers' horses, and you snatched her away.'

The Colonel rubbed his nose again and racked his memory. Indeed, he remembered the occasion now. A little thing with red hair and huge eyes, full of tears over a broken doll or some such thing. 'And she is now grown and in England?' he wondered aloud. 'And she is an actress?'

'One of a band of players roaming the countryside hereabouts,' Hunt affirmed. 'But you seem mighty interested in my affairs, Colonel. It is unlike you to concern yourself over the wenches with whom I may dally.'

Blood was not listening. He had risen from his chair and was surveying himself critically in the mirror.

'Well, I must away or I shall be late,' said Hunt, fastening on his cloak and picking up his riding crop.

'A moment,' said Blood quietly. 'Tell me, how old is the maid?'

'Some seventeen or eighteen years.'

'Too young to be my wife, would you say?'

Hunt dropped his riding crop in surprise and turned back to look at Blood, who was inspecting closely in the mirror the degree of greyness in his hair at the temples.

'Your wife?' Hunt repeated in astonishment. 'What the devil do you mean? You haven't ever clapped eyes on Kate. In any event, you are already married!'

'But Edith is far away in Lancashire, and I see her all too rarely.'

'She is a good wife to you – has borne you sons – why should you consider marrying again? And why a maid you have not met – and, moreover, one who is mine?'

Blood turned from the mirror, a smile lighting his dark eyes. 'Have no fear, Tom, I do not plan to marry your maid – or any other, for that matter. I simply wondered whether, in your view, the disparity in our ages would render it unlikely for your Kate to pass as my wife, that is all.'

'Pass as your wife?' Blood smiled to see the bewilderment change to dawning suspicion and understanding in the young man's eyes. 'Hold a moment – I begin to follow. You have another plan in mind, Colonel?'

Blood nodded sagely. 'I have a glimmering of an idea, and your little maid could well be of use to me. If, as you say, she is sympathetic to me and my dealings, she may well be willing to help in our next undertaking.'

'Of that I am certain, sir.'

'But we must be sure of her. Sound her out, Tom, and if she appears eager, then arrange for her to come here as soon as she is able. Then if I find her sincere, our next venture could well be the most exciting we have ever undertaken, Tom.'

Hunt sat down on the edge of a chair and leaned forward. 'Tell me, Colonel, what you have in mind.'

Blood shook his head. 'It is early yet, and I shall talk to none until I have the whole plan mapped out. But of this you can be sure – we shall go down to posterity for this deed.'

Hunt's eyes sparkled in anticipation. 'I would know more, but if you deem the moment unripe I am content to wait. We all have faith in you, Colonel.'

The Colonel smiled. 'But you had best make haste, Tom, if you are to meet your little witch, or the lady will tire of waiting and leave the Pheasant ere you reach there.'

Hunt leapt to his feet and snatched up his crop again. His handsome young face glowed with pleasure. 'I shall be all the more anxious to meet her now that I have occasion to try to induce her here,' he said. 'Fear not, I shall not fail you, Colonel. She will be here very soon.'

'I know,' murmured Blood confidently.

Gusts of warm air and merry laughter met Kate as she hurried into the Pheasant's welcoming doorway out of the cold night air, and she paused inside to look anxiously around for Dr Hunt's dark head. He was not there, not even in the gloom of the far window seat. Disappointment filled Kate. It was gone eight o'clock already. Perhaps he would not come after all.

She seated herself on the same settle as the night before, facing the door so he would be sure to see her as he entered. The landlord brought wine and Kate sat sipping hopefully. She saw Polly and another wench laughing and chatting with a group of men, and smiled back in answer to Polly's excited wave.

Time was passing. Suppose Hunt never came. Kate tried to brush away the feeling of disappointment. It was of little consequence if he did not come, she told herself firmly, but she knew that it was untrue. The sight of his dark, erect figure, tall and broadshouldered, had given rise to a tumult of feeling within her she had never known before, and she wished hard for him to appear.

Val's sullen face crossed her mind. He had dismissed her, cast her off as his wife for defying him tonight. She tossed her head angrily. Let him! But if Hunt was not to come after all, her defiance would have been all in vain. She sighed.

Time ticked on. Kate shifted on her seat to ease her legs. He was not coming now. Customers were beginning to call out their goodnights to the landlord, Polly and her friend among them, and trickle away into the darkness outside, and soon she would have to return, regretfully, to Val.

She rose stiffly and beckoned the landlord to settle the reckoning. As she did so, a sound of boots rang out loudly on the cobblestones outside and a tall figure appeared suddenly in the doorway, his eyes wide and anxious. It was Hunt. Kate's heart sang with delight.

A quick smile lit up his face when he saw her, and he strode swiftly towards her, taking both her hands in his. 'Kate! You are still here! I thought I had missed you. Forgive me, my dear, for being so wretchedly late, but my mare cast a shoe only half a mile from home and I could not risk riding her over that rough ground unshod.'

How thoughtful he was, even for an

animal. She gazed up at him, not attempting to disguise the evident pleasure in her eyes. It had not escaped her that he had called her Kate, and she was not in the least displeased by his familiarity. Hadn't she too been thinking of him as Tom?

He despatched the landlord to fetch more wine and meat pasty and drew Kate into the window seat. He tossed his cloak and plumed hat aside and sat close to her side, his dark eyes glowing with life and vigour, and Kate felt the warmth inside her responding to his liveliness.

He talked of his concern, both over the mare's shoe and that he might be too late in arriving at the inn. Then suddenly he took Kate's hands again.

'But you waited. I am so grateful that you did, Kate, for I could not blame a lady for growing tired of being kept dallying thus. But I should have been so distressed if you had gone.'

'What would you have done, sir?' Kate asked teasingly.

'I should have tracked you down without too much difficulty, I think, for a whole troupe of travelling players cannot hide so easily. Believe me, I would have traced you ere long for I would not easily let you go.'

He was turning her hands in his as he spoke. Suddenly his eyes clouded and he looked down. Kate felt ashamed of her roughened hands and made to draw them away. But it was not at her hands that he was looking, but at the cheap wedding ring on her finger. He looked up into her face again, his eyes troubled and perplexed.

Kate felt the blood slowly suffuse her cheeks, and she waited for the inevitable question.

TWELVE

Thomas Hunt did not mention Kate's ring nor question her, but went on talking quietly. Kate felt no anxiety to rush into explanation, and her embarrassment gradually faded as he pointedly ignored it and went on talking. But she sensed that his manner was decidedly cooler than before, and was sorry.

They parted at the lane end just as on the previous night and Kate was delighted when he lightly kissed her fingertips as they stood by the stile.

'I shall remain at the Pheasant tonight,' Hunt said softly, 'and have Bess re-shod in the morning. May I see you again to-morrow?'

Kate's spirits lifted. Married or not he wanted to see her again, and she him. Having assured him she would be there the following evening she hastened back to the mill, not casting a backward glance despite the temptation to have a last glimpse of his big, broad figure.

Val was snoring loudly when she crept down beside him, and he was still sleeping deeply when she rose again in the morning. Alida was standing by the camp fire, stretching and yawning sleepily.

'How did you fare last night?' she demanded of Kate in a bored voice. 'Did you earn us more money?'

'No,' Kate admitted.

Alida's eyebrows rose. 'Ah, your client tired of you quickly, did he not? Could you not procure yourself another from among the yokels at the inn?'

Kate flushed angrily. It was all very well for Alida to sneer, safe as she was from the task of earning money for the band. But Alida had yet another victory to announce.

'It is of little import, however,' she drawled

163

languidly, 'for I think the company will surely disband soon and it will be for each to earn his own bread then.'

'Disband?' Kate echoed. 'Has Charles decided so then?'

Alida smiled. 'He soon will. He and I are to be married, you know.' She patted her rounded stomach with satisfaction. 'I fancy Charles will do as I ask him, once we are wed. He seeks only to please me.'

'And Constance?'

'Oh – her!' Alida's voice was thick with scorn. 'The sooner I can find a husband for her, the better. Marry her off and let her bear some fellow a dozen more yokels for his farm, that is the best plan for her.'

She snatched her skirts round angrily and paced quickly away. The mention of Constance had irritated her too much to want to continue the conversation, Kate could see. She had not even waited to score off Kate over her forthcoming marriage.

Kate busied herself helping Constance prepare the company's main meal of the day, cutting up vegetables and pieces of chicken to add to the stew in the pot. Not once did Val appear. He was apparently sleeping or simply lying on his bed of straw, unwilling to come out. Very well, thought

Kate, if he wants to snub me and sulk, then let him!

But before she left for the inn, Kate decided to go to him. After all, there were matters to discuss. If Alida carried out her threat to have the troupe disbanded, then Kate and Val must plan what they should do.

Val sat crouched, his arms about his knees, on a pile of straw. He glowered when he saw her approach.

'You have not eaten, Val,' Kate commented. 'Everyone else has dined well tonight.'

'I do not wish to eat,' he growled.

Kate shrugged. 'As you wish, but sullen brooding will gain you naught,' she added drily. Val remained silent. 'Alida tells me she will have Charles disband the company soon,' she went on.

Val jerked his shoulders angrily. 'She may do as she pleases. I care naught. You can all go to Hades!'

Kate sighed and decided to persist. 'Val, be reasonable,' she said gently. 'We must plan what we are to do.'

Val turned sharply to face her, his face hard and his eyes glittering with an unnatural light. 'Get out!' he snarled in a

165

low, menacing voice. 'Get away from me! Go away and do not come back! I hate the sight of you, Kate Varney, and I never wish to see you again!'

'Val, please!' Kate hastened to kneel beside him, but he flung out his arm and pushed her off-balance. She sprawled in the straw, gazing up at him in disbelief.

'You heard me, mistress!' he hissed. 'Get you hence, where you will, but do not come near me again. I want no part of you!' He turned savagely away and began muttering to himself. Kate rose slowly.

'Very well,' she said quietly, and turned to go. He was behaving very oddly, she mused. He was often sullen and hasty in his words but never before so savage as this. He looked flushed and strange too. Was he truly ill, as he had claimed? Or did he honestly wish to be rid of her? She could still hear him moaning 'Get out, go away,' as he rocked to and fro.

A figure leaning against the barn door uncurled and straightened up as Kate made to go out. It was Alida. She must have overheard some of their conversation, for she smiled broadly.

'So, Valentine has no further use for you? I chanced to overhear.'

'Eavesdropper! Perchance it was you who put him up to this?' Kate countered angrily.

'I?' echoed Alida in mild tones. 'Why no, it is his own wish entirely.' She stood aside to let Kate pass, then followed her curiously. 'What will you do now, Kate? Where can you turn now for protection? Oh, you poor creature! I do so pity you with no husband or even a lover to protect you.'

Kate turned angrily, her eyes flashing fire. 'You – pity me! There is no need, I assure you, mistress. I am well able to care for myself, now as always.'

Alida watched her closely. 'You will leave here then?' she asked almost unbelievingly.

Kate smiled grimly. 'Aye, you win, Alida. You sought once before to be rid of me, did you not?'

'I did? When?' Alida's eyes were innocently wide.

'When you set the barn afire.'

Alida's eyelids flickered a moment before her face resumed its air of innocent bewilderment. 'I know not what you mean, Kate. But I am concerned for you now. Have you some plan?'

Kate faltered. She had no plan except to meet Tom Hunt tonight, and she was not going to speak of him to Alida. 'No,' she murmured, and saw Alida's malicious smile of triumph. 'But I shall devise some means, have no fear.'

It was time to go. Kate purposefully drew off her wedding ring once Alida had sauntered gracefully away, and put it into her bodice. Now in truth she was no longer wed.

Hunt was sitting in the inn waiting, his eyes on the door watching for her. He waved and came through the throng of customers to meet her and drew her into the corner, his dark face glowing. In his long tunic of deep red velvet with its many buttons and fine lace ruffles he looked exceedingly handsome and impressive, and Kate trembled with pleasure. As they supped and ate he talked animatedly.

'Kate, you are not listening to me,' he said eventually, a gentle note of accusation in his voice.

'I am sorry. You were speaking of a new business venture, I believe?' She had been lost in admiration of him. She looked up now and saw he was gazing at her earnestly.

'Oh Kate, I have been trying to lead up subtly to what I really want to say, and you haven't been listening to a word.'

'I was preoccupied. But if you have aught to say, why not come straight to the point?'

He laughed. 'Ever the direct, honest maid I took you for. I am trying to ask you to come away with me, Kate. Will you come?'

He took both her hands in his and gazed directly at her. Kate thought she had never seen such an open, frank expression in any man's eyes, and her heart bounded. She was eager to go with him wherever he went, but before she could open her lips to reply, he spoke again.

'No ring,' he commented. 'I could swear that yesterday you carried a ring upon your wedding finger, but now I see it is gone. What does that signify, Kate?'

Kate blushed. She was at a loss how to answer for a moment, and then she decided to parry his question. 'Lud, sir, I do not quiz you upon your rings,' she quipped, and glanced at his hands. For the first time she noticed that he wore a ring with a huge dark-green stone streaked with red and set in a wide band of gold.

'There is no mystery about my ring,' Hunt replied. 'It was given me by my father many years ago. A bloodstone, from India, he told me.'

Kate caught her breath. A bloodstone! She

had expected a stone as red as blood as its name implied, not deep green like the depths of a stagnant pool. She thought again of the gipsy at her wedding, how she had spoken of a bloodstone and a tall, dark man who would play an important part in Kate's life. The old crone had spoken of a fire and death and of crossing water – and all this had already come true, and now the man with the bloodstone had come into her life. It could not be mere coincidence. The old woman had certainly had the gift of second sight.

Kate looked into Tom Hunt's eyes. A gentle smile played about his lips and irradiated his eyes, and Kate's heart lurched. Yes, she must go with this man. Val had dismissed her and never wanted to see her again, so the path was clear.

'Well?' Hunt murmured at last. 'I have need of you, Kate. There are great schemes afoot and you will be invaluable to me. And what is more, not only to me.' He glanced about him and lowered his voice. 'If you wish, you could aid your hero, Colonel Blood, too.'

Kate sat upright. 'Blood?' she echoed.

'Hush!' Hunt patted her hands. 'It is dangerous even to speak his name. But if you wished it, Kate, I could take you to him. Perchance you could be of use to him too.'

Kate rose at once. 'Take me to him,' she said simply. 'I shall go wherever you go.'

Without a word Hunt settled the bill and strode out into the yard, calling for the ostler. A bedraggled youth, shivering inside his threadbare coat, led out Hunt's grey mare and pulled his forelock gratefully when a couple of groats were put into his frozen hand. Hunt helped Kate to mount, then climbed up behind her and set off at a trot.

It was exciting to feel his arms around her as he held the reins and the warmth of his body close behind her. The cold night air whipped her cheeks and added to the mounting exultation inside her. As the trees slipped by, grey as ghosts in the gloom, Kate felt she was leaving her old way of life far behind, and she experienced a tremendous thrill of anticipation of the new. With this strong, gentle man beside her, she was happy.

Frost-carpeted fields at length gave way to rutted roads leading into a small town, and Hunt reined in his horse at the gate of a house on the outskirts.

'Rochford, Kate, and home. Come.' He

dismounted and held out his hands to her. Kate slid down into his waiting arms and wondered. For a brief moment he held her close, then released her to go and ring the bell. A woman came scurrying.

'Doctor Ayliffe is abed, Mr Hunt,' she said as they entered, and Kate saw her curious stare of appraisal.

'No matter. Prepare a room for the lady, mistress, for she will be my guest for some time.'

The woman scurried off again, her slippered feet flapping on the stone floor.

'Will you eat?' Hunt asked Kate when they were alone in a booklined study, warm and fragrant with the scent of pomanders.

'Thank you, no. I have eaten well tonight.'

He poured out two glasses of brandy, and as they sat and sipped it before the low fire the woman returned to say she had aired a bed and the chamber was ready.

'Go to bed now, Kate,' Hunt urged her gently, 'and when you have slept well we shall talk more in the morning. Good night, my dear, and sleep sweetly.'

It was sheer bliss for Kate to climb between the warm, clean sheets of a four-poster bed. Never since she had worked in the Lennie household in Ireland had she slept in a bed with sheets and blankets on it. And never once had she slept in a huge bed like this, but only in a low truckle bed. This was fine living indeed, and if it was a sign of how life was to be for her from now on, she would never regret having made her choice to leave the company and go with Hunt.

She drifted into a deep and comfortable sleep, her mind still pondering over what Val would do now and what Hunt's plans for her might be.

Next morning she was awake and dressed early, and went downstairs. The house-keeper showed her into a chamber where Tom Hunt was already at breakfast. He rose and came to meet her.

'Come and eat, Kate. Soon Dr Ayliffe will be down and I'd like to present you to him.'

Kate ate slowly, savouring the bacon and beans and wondering what part this Dr Ayliffe played in Tom's life. Was he, too, a supporter of Colonel Blood?

As Tom chatted to her across the table, Kate heard the door open. Tom dropped his napkin and smiled broadly. 'Ah, here he is. Doctor, I should like you to meet Mistress Kate Varney. Kate – may I present Doctor Ayliffe.'

Kate rose and advanced to meet the

elderly gentleman, then stood, transfixed. The genial face with the dark eyes and long nose was smiling at her thoughtfully, but Kate felt a sudden stab of surprise, of recollection. He was familiar to her, and yet she could not quite place him. The once-dark hair, now crisply grey at the temples, and the bushy eyebrows that practically met over the large nose seemed like an ill-painted image of a face she had once known, but where? And when?

She held out her hand stiffly and the thoughtful face creased into a smile. At once the dark eyes lit up and seemed positively to twinkle as he took her outstretched finger-tips and bowed to kiss them. Kate cried out.

'I have it now! You are he, the black crow!'

The doctor stopped and straightened. 'I beg your pardon, Mistress Varney?'

'You are not Dr Ayliffe, but Colonel Blood!'

The old man's wide eyes narrowed and he smiled again at young Hunt. 'You were right, Tom. She is shrewd. I congratulate you, mistress, on your fine memory. I am delighted to meet you again, Kate Varney, but I swear that but for the red hair I should never have known you, such a beauty you have grown.' His voice was warm and had a soft Irish inflection that reminded Kate of home.

He bent and this time he kissed her hand. Hunt was beaming with pleasure. Kate re-seated herself and Blood sat between the young couple and began helping himself liberally to food. Kate could scarcely believe it. Here she was, sitting at table with a living legend, the notorious Colonel Blood him-self, and he looked as innocuous as any elderly gentleman could.

He smiled gravely. 'So Tom was able to persuade you to join us, I take it. I presume then that you are in sympathy with my aims.'

'I know little of your aims, sir, but I have heard of your exploits all my life and regarded you with respect as every Irishman does. I shall be happy to be of service to you in any way I can.'

'Good, that is good,' Blood murmured round a mouthful of food. 'Then I hope you will be happy with us, and in time I shall tell you what I plan. But for the moment, simply enjoy yourself with young Tom here. In the meantime, I pray you do not call me by my name, but Dr Ayliffe, for as such am I known here.'

He bent again to the task of eating, and

Kate could see he was content that his wish would be fulfilled, for he did not wait to see whether she agreed. He was obviously a man accustomed to giving orders and to having them obeyed without question.

She watched him curiously. He was no longer a huge black crow that swept down on her from nowhere, but still a tall, impressive figure of a man, broad shoulders giving the impression of suppressed strength even as he ate. But his placid countenance gave no hint of the evil-wreaking miscreant people held him to be. Only the humorous glint in his eye betokened the fiery nature within. And it was his eyes, deep and dark and mysterious, that Kate remembered so well from that day in her childhood when she was carried along the Dublin alleys.

She came out of her reverie. Blood and Tom Hunt were talking of the day's work, and then Blood rose to leave.

'I must go visit one of my patients,' he told them. 'But Tom may amuse you, show you our still room and explain what we do.'

Kate was content to be left in Tom Hunt's care. He led her to the little laboratory where he and Blood prepared the medicaments for their patients, and Kate was bemused by the list of potions and salves,

clysters and draughts, simples and com-
pounds that he told her they concocted
there. A mortar and pestle and an iron
crucible lay upon a long bench and row
upon row of jars and bottles filled high
shelves. The jars contained, so Tom told her,
for Kate could not read the labels, oils and
essences, antimony, benzoar and valerian,
wormwood, thyme, rosemary and many
other substances of which Kate had never
heard before. It seemed like magic, to be
able to concoct cures for all ills from
ingredients such as these. She commented
so to Tom, and he threw back his head and
laughed.

'Magic? The devil's work, more like,' he
chuckled. 'Some of our potions may be
efficacious, but others are simply harmless
substances which avail naught. But it keeps
our patients content to be dosed with a
placebo or purged, and it keeps our pockets
filled.'

Kate looked at him wonderingly. 'Then
you deliberately cheat your patients?' she
asked.

'Not we. We do what we can. I know
something of the apothecary's trade, having
once been apprenticed for a time, but
neither Blood nor I is licensed to dispense

as an apothecary. Simples may be distilled by anyone and many a housewife performs this task for her household. We simply charge a fee to the villagers who require our services.'

He was watching her reaction closely. Kate smiled. After all, it was no more deceitful to sell useless potions than to steal, as she had often done.

'And in truth,' Tom added, as he closed the door behind them, 'this is but a temporary way of life until the Colonel gives us the order to begin our next campaign. When he gives the signal, we shall close the house and away.'

Kate wondered then just how long it would be until Blood gave the order, and what the plan would be. Most of all she wondered what her part in the affair would be.

THIRTEEN

The next few days passed in a pleasant haze of diversion for Kate, browsing around the house or indulging herself to the full, leaning on the bench, chin in hands, watching Tom preparing potions and syrups, pounding away with his pestle and mortar or pouring carefully-measured liquids into a dish.

It was a pleasant, lazy life for Kate with no duties to perform about the house, nothing to do but gaze at Tom's handsome, genial face as he hummed at his work. It was Blood, or rather Dr Ayliffe as she must remember to call him, who saw to most of the patients who came to the house, and she was free to enjoy Tom's company to the full.

Only occasionally did a guilty flicker cross her mind of the husband she had abandoned. But then the memory of Val's forceful words when he had told her to go, never to return, softened the guilt and she tossed her head defiantly. She was as free as if she were a widow, so why concern herself overmuch with Valentine now? He, no doubt, would have found Constance willing to comfort him by now, and as for Kate … well, it was evident that Tom was glad to have her close by him while he worked, and she was content. Just to watch his athletic, broad-shouldered figure and his abstracted air of concentration as he bent to his task, made her quiver with excitement.

Every now and again Tom raised his dark

head and smiled a slow, leisurely smile that caused Kate to shudder with delight. This, she felt sure, was the true, delicious sensation of love, the rapture she had always yearned for and never found before. This was a man she could respect and admire, a man to whose will she would be glad to submit her own, fiery as she was.

Slowly, almost reluctantly, Kate realised she must indeed be falling in love with him, for who else in the world could dictate to Kate Varney? But for Tom Hunt she knew she would go to the ends of the world and never hesitate to ask why.

It was on the evening of the third day that Kate and Tom met Blood coming out of his study, a sheaf of papers in his hand. He looked serious and tight-lipped and he stood for a moment and surveyed Kate with a close, scrutinising look.

'I am for London soon, Kate, and Tom must go with me. We shall close up the house and settle in lodgings I have arranged.'

Tom took a step forward. 'Then your plans are complete, sir? May I know the details?'

Kate saw the eager light in his eye, but saw it die again as quickly when Blood shook his head. 'I can tell you naught save that we shall meet Parrett and Holloway in London. More I cannot reveal yet. Much depends on whether or not Kate will come with us.' He looked down at her and spoke softly. 'Will you come, Kate? The plan I have conceived will hinge largely on your help. Can I count on you?'

The dark eyes bored into her own and held her mesmerised. It was difficult for Kate to break the hold of his hypnotic gaze and turn to look at Tom, to see how he reacted, but Tom's attention was solely for the Colonel. He stood eager and wide-eyed, as if trying to read Blood's plan in his expression. That settled it, Kate decided. If Tom was willing to follow blindly wherever this man led, then what need had she to hesitate. Tom had been involved with Blood in his secret activities often before, and he obviously had no fear or hesitation in gladly falling in with him again.

'I shall be honoured to join you, sir,' she said soberly. The older man smiled benevolently and patted her shoulder.

'Let me tell you simply that the plan I conceive will not distress you, Kate. As a true Irish patriot you will approve the action though you may not appreciate the reason.'

'It is to be soon then, Colonel, if we are to leave for London immediately?'

The Colonel shook his head slowly from side to side. 'Not so hasty, Tom. There is yet much to plan and prepare for, and it may take weeks before we are ready. But to begin with, we must fit Kate out with new clothes to suit her part.'

Kate looked up, her eyes glistening at the prospect of new apparel. Clothes of her very own, not gowns shared by many wenches from the common hamper of costumes the travelling players owned.

'Yes,' Blood went on thoughtfully, 'it were best you were fitted out in London, for if I call in the local dressmaker to make gowns and cloaks for you here, the whole village would soon be babbling with gossip, and it would be thought for certain that the old doctor had got himself a mistress.'

Tom smiled with amusement, but Kate turned aside to hide the flush that reddened her cheeks. Her embarrassment, however, was soon forgotten when she lay abed revelling in the prospect of new cloaks and a new, exciting life in London. What kind of gowns would Blood order for her, she wondered. Would they be fine silks and satins, velvet or moire, as befitted a lady? Or

– her heart sank at the possibility – merely stuffs and worsted suited to a working wench? It all depended on what role he had in mind for her. Oh, please, she begged Providence inwardly, let it be a lady! I could play the part well, and I do so long to wear a fine gown, sprigged with lace and finely embroidered!

As she lay in bed, sleepless with excitement and turning over the possibilities in her mind, Kate heard footsteps on the gravel path outside, and then the sound of the bell as someone pulled the bell rope. Voices muttered urgently, a brief silence, and the footsteps then sounded on the gravel again.

Kate rose and peered curiously out of the latticed window. In the gloom below a cloaked figure stood waiting while Blood led his horse out from the stables. The figure moved towards him.

'How far away did you say it was, mistress?' Blood's voice demanded as he mounted the horse. Kate could not hear the murmured reply. 'Then I shall go ahead and you may follow,' he said, and cantered off down the lane.

The cloaked figure looked upwards, and as she did so the hood of her cloak fell back, revealing a glimpse of a woman's blonde head before she too set off down the lane. Odd, thought Kate, but the glimpse reminded her forcibly of Constance. But that was impossible. The players were several miles away. It could not possibly have been her.

She climbed back into the tester bed and fell soundly asleep. In the morning she breakfasted with Tom. Blood did not appear, and after a time Kate enquired about him.

'He was called out to see a sick man late last night and has not yet returned,' Tom told her. 'But do not fret, he knows what time the London coach leaves the inn, and his bags are already packed. He will return in time.'

But the time for the coach's departure drew near and still the Colonel had not come. Kate felt uneasy, though Tom supervised the loading of all the trunks with apparent unconcern.

'I know the Colonel, Kate, and I know he will come.'

But the coach was almost ready to leave before Blood arrived, tired and dishevelled, at the inn. He dined quickly of cold meat and ale and climbed aboard the coach, seating himself wearily opposite Kate and Tom.

Soon the coach heaved and lumbered off along the rutted lanes. As it jolted slowly along, Tom eyed the Colonel with amusement.

'You live your part as the physician to the bitter end, Colonel. You could not resist a worried wife's desperate plea even on the eve of forsaking your physician's life.'

Blood laughed, but there was little amusement in the sound. 'She had cause to worry, my friend, for the man was sorely ill. I could do but little to relieve his suffering. They were players, he and the woman, Kate,' he added, turning his dark eyes on her, 'strolling players newly arrived and camping some two miles out of the village. I wondered if they might be your friends for I noted their voices had an Irish accent.'

Kate caught her breath. Then it *was* Constance she had seen below her window last night. In that event, who was the sick man, for Constance had no husband. She asked Blood if he knew the name of his patient.

'I did not pause to enquire,' Blood answered slowly and reflectively, 'for the man was suffering desperately.'

'Then you can send him no bill,' Tom pointed out.

Blood shook his head. 'The woman told me when she came that she had no money, but begged me to help nonetheless, for the poor creature was in agony. Wait – I have it now – I heard the woman soothing him as he cried and moaned, and I'm sure she addressed him as Valentine.'

Kate lurched forward, a sick feeling of fear and guilt clutching her throat. Tom's hand caught her arm and steadied her.

'Take care now, 'tis always a bumpy ride over these cursed, uneven lanes,' he murmured.

'Stop the coach!' Kate cried, near to hysteria and full of guilt at what she had done. 'I must go back! I must go to help Val!'

She leapt to her feet and searched desperately about for some means to attract the coachman's attention. Tom sat agape, but Blood took her arm. 'Sit down again, Kate,' he commanded quietly.

'But I *must* go!' Kate cried again, and she could feel the tears beginning to scald her eyelids. Blood's grip was still firm on her arm.

'Be seated, Kate,' he said again. The note

of authority in his voice was not to be denied. Kate sat down beside Tom and stared stupidly at Blood. He leaned towards her. 'Whatever this man may have meant to you, my dear, be assured that your going to him now would avail him naught – nor you either.'

'I – I – don't understand you,' Kate whimpered.

'Then I'll explain. He was sick of the plague, Kate, the plague that puts the fear of God in every man. Already most of the company had recognised the signs and they had fled – the company manager and his wife and all the actors. Only this Constance stayed by him.'

Kate stared at him in disbelief. The plague! She shuddered involuntarily for she had seen victims of the plague in Ireland and knew the terrible, tormenting carbuncles that it caused and the agonising death, often preceded by madness, that it brought in its train. And Val had no one but Constance who cared a jot about him. She *must* go back!

Kate gathered her confused wits and removed the Colonel's restraining hand from her arm.

'Colonel Blood,' she said quietly now, 'I

am sorry to have to disturb your plans, but it is my duty to return. You see, Valentine is my husband.'

She dared not look to see the reaction on Tom's face, but she knew he would be bewildered by her disclosure. It was unfortunate for she would have followed him anywhere, and now it would be impossible, but she must do as her conscience directed.

Keeping her face averted from Tom, she looked hard into Blood's sober eyes. 'You do understand, Colonel, do you not?'

Blood nodded thoughtfully. 'But it is too late, Kate. There would be no point in your going now, nor indeed for a physician for that matter.'

Kate's heart fluttered. 'What do you mean?'

'I mean just that – it is too late. Despite the woman's pleadings, there was nothing I could do for him. I worked all night lancing the carbuncles that caused him to rave so, cooling his fever as best as I could, but it was useless. By the time I left he was unconscious, and unless I am sorely mistaken, he had but a few hours of gasping left, and by now it is done.'

Kate turned unbelieving eyes towards Tom. He leaned forwards and took Kate's trembling hands in his own.

'It were best you leave matters be, Kate, and do as the Colonel says,' he murmured.

Kate could not help it. The lump in her throat resolved itself into a sudden flood of tears, tears of shame and guilt. Tom's arm encircled her shoulders comfortingly and the two men sat in silence while the coach bumped on its way and Kate's tears flowed unrestrainedly.

FOURTEEN

London was confusion to Kate. It was dark by the time the coach disgorged its passengers in the cobbled yard of the Black Bull, but despite the lateness of the hour the streets were alive with activity. All around the inn-yard poorly-clad men jostled to get through the crowd of tarts and prostitutes, anxious to earn a groat by carrying the travellers' bags. The innkeeper strode out from the lighted doorway of his tavern and shouted angrily to them to get hence and not to harass his patrons.

Blood, however, was not prepared to

accept mine host's invitation to dine and sleep there the night. He shook his head firmly.

'I shall call a hackney to take us to our lodgings, where we are expected,' he told Kate and Tom, and before long the hackney was trundling along London's cobbled streets and over the river.

Kate by now was too sleepy to arouse much interest in Tom's remarks as to where they were. London streets looked very much like the Dublin streets she remembered from childhood, with sedan chairs carrying passengers to and fro, and linkboys lighting the way for pedestrians. She wondered how far they still had to travel, and how long it would be before she could sleep, for she was utterly exhausted and aching in every bone from the long coach journey. By now she had shed so many tears over Val that her eyes were sore and her throat ached.

At last Blood called out to the coachman to stop, and Tom helped Kate to alight. Blood ushered them quickly into a small house, one of a row of similar small houses with overhanging upper storeys in a narrow dark street. The air, both in the street and in the little, gloomy house, smelt foetid and unwholesome, and Kate could not resist wrinkling her nose in distaste. Blood noticed her expression and smiled.

'Whitefriars might not be the pleasantest spot in London, I admit, Kate, but at least we are among friends here,' he commented, and turned to meet the old woman who padded out to meet them.

The old dame grunted laconically in answer to Blood's murmured questions, and showed them upstairs to their rooms, panting with difficulty as she mounted the narrow stairs before them. Kate's little chamber lay between Blood's and Tom's, and she cast scarcely a glance at the sparse furnishings and the cheap coverings on the truckle bed before flinging herself full-length on the bed, fully-dressed, and falling into a deep sleep of sheer exhaustion.

In the morning she was awoken by a girl's high-pitched giggle in the next room, followed by squeals and shrieks, and then the sound of running footsteps. The door of Kate's room burst open, and a girl of about her own age, flushed and bright-eyed, stood on the threshold. She was very pretty, Kate thought, with her rich brown hair falling in abundant, curly masses over her shoulders, although her dressing-gown was rather shabby and threadbare.

Kate sat up. She was conscious of the fact that she must present a very grimy and unattractive picture, still in her travel-stained gown and with her face unwashed. The girl did not seem to notice. She hovered hesitantly at the doorway.

'Oh,' she said, and the look of disappointment on her face was all that she offered by way of apology for her intrusion. 'Isn't Tom here? I thought this was his room!'

Her face was creased in puzzlement. Kate swung her legs off the side of the bed and stood up.

'He is next door,' she told the girl, 'but which side of me I do not know.' She did not add that she had just heard the girl running from the room to the right, but presumably she knew who was the occupant there.

The girl's frown disappeared, and her face lighted up. 'Ah, in that case he is here, for Doctor Ayliffe is in that chamber. I have just left him.'

Kate was surprised by her cool announcement, but could not fail to notice her rather coarse, rough-edged voice. At the same moment she became aware of other sounds she had failed to notice until now – the high pitched, insistent wail of a baby in another house, the rattle of dishes and the cries of traders in the street below.

The girl was still watching Kate curiously. With complete lack of self-consciousness she stood there staring, her dressing-gown agape, and eventually she lowered herself on the edge of the bed.

'You with them?' she asked.

'Who?'

'With Tom and Doctor Ayliffe. Did they bring you here?'

'Yes.'

Kate was embarrassed by her questioning, and feared lest she might probe too much. The girl nodded approvingly.

'I see. I'm Bess,' she said, as if that explained all.

Kate turned away, looking for a bowl of water to rinse her face, but there was none to be found in the little chamber. Who was this girl? Was she Blood's doxy, or Tom's for that matter, since she had asked for him?

The girl Bess produced an apple from somewhere and began crunching it noisily. 'You just out of Newgate?'

'Newgate?' Kate repeated, bewildered.

'Not Newgate? You're not a debtor then. Well, let me guess.' The girl rolled her eyes ceilingwards and pondered as she crunched. 'I have it! You are with child and have been run out of your parish! That's it, and Tom and the Colonel – doctor, I mean – took pity on you. I'll warrant that's it. Ever the kind-hearted ones, they are.'

Kate whipped round angrily. 'I am not with child,' she exclaimed. 'And what right have you, may I ask, to pry into my affairs, I'd like to know?'

Bess threw back her head and laughed, pieces of apple gleaming in her teeth. 'Lord, you haven't been here long,' she commented between chuckles, 'or you'd know we don't have secrets from each other here in Alsatia. Thieves and rogues every one of us, but honest enough in our own way.'

'Where? Alsatia?' Kate repeated wonderingly. Blood had called this place White-friars.

It was Bess's turn to look surprised. 'You haven't heard of Alsatia?' she murmured. 'Yet you were brought here. People only come here for safety from the law, that much I do know, people who've escaped from Newgate or are wanted as rum-pads or some such. If you're not wanted, why have they brought you here?'

Kate could not understand the girl at all now, with her talk of rum-pads. She looked at her sharply. 'What are you talking about?

I am no criminal, if that is what you are implying. I don't even know what a rum-pad is.'

The girl sat up attentively and a suspicious look clouded her hazel eyes. 'Rum-pads are highwaymen, everyone knows that. And like I said, people only come here for sanctuary from the law – or to spy. But spies don't live long. The Colonel sees to that. He's tried several and had them hanged before now. So if you're here on false pretences, let me warn you now, mistress, that Alsatia isn't healthy for the likes of you.'

She stood up, clearing Kate's head by a couple of inches. 'If you've cozened Tom and the doctor into bringing you here in the hope of earning a shilling or two from the government for your information, then the best piece of advice I can give you is to clear out, fast, before the others find out. It's a long time since we saw a woman strung up, and I reckon the citizens of Alsatia would relish the sight.'

Before Kate could overcome her astonishment Bess had flung swiftly out of the room, and Kate heard her go into the next room and slam the door. Hushed voices carried on a lengthy conversation, but what words Kate might have managed to make out were drowned by the ever-growing clamour in the street outside.

Kate looked out of the little, dusty-paned window. The little alley was so narrow that she could scarcely see into the street below, but in the windows of the little houses opposite she could see women shaking out bedding or emptying slop-pails into the street with a cry of 'Gardey loo!' Infants' cries still shrilled in the stench-laden air and people below wrangled and cursed noisily. Kate had never heard such noise in such a confined area in her life.

The door opened and Kate turned. Tom stood leaning lazily against the door post, his arm draped affectionately across Bess's shoulders. Kate could see the gleam of the bloodstone ring on his hand as it lay on the girl's shoulders, and she felt angry resentment rising in her throat. Was Bess a close friend of Tom's, or even more than that? She was obviously in the confidence of both Tom and Blood, for had she not inadvertently referred to Blood as the colonel? Kate felt jealous and angry.

Tom was smiling good-naturedly. 'I have heard of your little contretemps with Bess, Kate, and I have explained to her that you are one of us, and completely trustworthy. I

196

hope that now you two will be friends, for Colonel Blood will brook no sparring and fighting in the ranks.'

So the girl was in their confidence, for Tom himself did not try to hide Blood's name. Kate saw that Bess was regarding her still somewhat suspiciously. Tom waited for one girl or the other to hold out a sign of peace, but neither girl moved.

'Let us go down to breakfast, Tom,' Bess said at length, and taking Tom's arm firmly she drew him out. Kate blazed with anger. The girl was obviously trying to prove her superiority, her prior involvement with the men, and her power over Tom. Kate fumed. Let her wait! Kate would cook her goose for her, some day, but as yet she knew not how.

Finding no water to wash, Kate cleaned her face of the journey's dust with spit and the hem of her gown, then smoothed her hair as best she could and went down the narrow, rickety stairs. She could hear Blood's low-toned but commanding voice, its soft, Irish lilt giving Kate a twinge of nostalgia. She turned the door knob of the room whence his voice came, and went in.

Blood and Tom and the girl were already eating heartily at a long, deal table which still bore the empty tankards and spilled ale of last night. The whole chamber was dusty and in disorder, as if the housekeeper was of too slatternly a frame of mind to care. Of the old woman who had admitted them to the house last night there was no sign.

'Come, sit and eat,' Tom invited her cheerily, and he drew out a chair next to himself. Bess sat on his other side, chewing noisily on a hunk of cold beef.

'You have already met my Bess, I believe,' Colonel Blood said with a smile to Kate as he pushed the platter of meat towards her. Kate nodded. She had heard Bess emerge from Blood's chamber that morning, but she still did not know how the girl stood with him. Such a coarse creature could not be his wife surely?

Blood seemed to read her thoughts as he sat swilling his ale thoughtfully round the tankard and watching her closely from under his thick eyebrows. 'Bess is my good friend,' he explained slowly. 'She knows my wife is sick and far away, but she always prepares a good welcome for me in London as any good wife would. She has our chambers aired and in readiness, and horses and whatever else we may require. A sound, reliable wench, are you not, my Bess?'

The girl looked up from the meat in her

hands, and Kate could see the loving, approving look in her eyes.

'I am here and ready whenever you want me, Colonel,' she said quietly, then went back to her chewing.

'It is good to have trustworthy friends,' Blood murmured, 'but sometimes it is hard to know who are friends and who are dissemblers.'

The girl grunted. 'You've made short shrift of those you've found out to be spies,' she commented. 'Last time you came it was William Boar, remember? The watchman found him hanging from the barber's pole after your court had found him guilty, and I reckon that served as a warning to many another who might have thought to play foul with you. Now there's very few who dare cross Colonel Blood.'

Kate felt certain that Bess was recounting this tale for her benefit, for it was obvious the girl distrusted her. Blood apparently was not slow to catch her meaning either.

'Kate is a trusted friend, Bess, and you shall treat her so.'

Bess buried her teeth deeper into the meat without even a glance at Kate, but Kate could feel her dislike reaching out to her. Was the girl jealous? Tom's arm lay idly along the back of Kate's chair – was Bess perhaps jealous on his account? She was obviously Blood's doxy and willing follower, but who was to know whether she did not prefer Blood's handsome young lieutenant?

When they had all finished eating, Blood suggested that Tom should take Kate out to see the district. 'But keep within the confines of Alsatia,' he warned them before they left. 'It may not be the most salubrious part of London, but it is certainly the safest for the time being.'

Tom walked close by Kate's side, his hand cupped under her elbow, and for that Kate was very grateful. On all sides they were pressed and harried by pedlars and beggars, street traders and cripples and starved-looking children.

'Beware of pickpockets,' Tom warned her, and almost as he spoke he was almost knocked off his feet by a hurtling youth who cannoned into him. The boy murmured and turned to run off, but Tom grabbed him by the ear.

'Give it back,' he commanded firmly.

'Give what back, guv?' the youth protested, yelping as Tom tweaked his ear.

'Whatever it was you just took,' Tom said. The boy kept yelping and twisting, but Tom held on firmly. Finally the boy dragged out a linen handkerchief from under the back of his ragged coat, and Tom let him go. The lad disappeared into the crowd.

Tom laughed as he put the handkerchief into his pocket again. 'An old trick,' he commented, 'but no longer one that fools me.'

Kate liked the humorous gleam in his warm, dark eyes. He was a kindly man, she thought, for he could have handed the youth over to the constable. She asked him why he had not. Tom threw back his head and roared.

'No constable or bailiff ever dares set foot in Alsatia, Kate, 'tis more than his life is worth. There is no justice here but rough justice. That, my Kate, is why we are here, for we are out of reach of the law.'

'It is a vile, stinking place,' Kate commented, grimacing as they picked their way through rotting piles of refuse and manure. 'How long shall we stay here, Tom?'

'Till the Colonel is ready.' Tom set his lips firmly and said no more, and Kate did not question him further. He, like Bess, would accept Blood's orders and act on them implicitly, without question or demur. And so would she.

They went back to the house in the little

alley and found the old housekeeper in the hallway.

'Kate, this is Mistress Millichope, the proprietor of the establishment,' Tom introduced her.

'Is she a new girl?' the beldame grunted, her sparse eyebrows raised in question as she looked Kate over.

'No indeed, mistress, she is not for your troupe but for me and the Colonel personally,' Tom told her, and again Kate could detect the gleam of amusement in his eyes.

The old woman pinched Kate's arm. 'Mmm,' she grunted, 'keep the best for yerself, don't yer?' and she ambled off down the dark hallway to the rear of the house.

'What did she mean?' Kate could not resist the question. Tom smiled.

'Mistress Millichope's establishment is a bawdy house, Kate, and she hoped such a fine, firm, pretty wench as you were being offered to her to add to her team of fillies.'

Kate turned this over in her mind. 'And Bess?'

'Bess is her prime attraction. But when the Colonel is here, she is for his use exclusively. Blood pays liberally for whatever he wants, and Mistress Millichope is not fool enough to decline his gold. So while Bess is unavailable, I think she hoped for another beauty like you to replace her.'

Kate shuddered at the thought. True, she had been prepared to sell herself when she had first met Tom at the Pheasant, but then it would have been to a client of her own choosing. In a bawdy house she would be accessible to anyone who took a fancy to her, thief or cripple, young or old. It was a gruesome thought. She began to think less harshly of Bess now.

The next few days passed without any new excitement for Kate. Blood was busy with paper and pen, writing and sealing letters which he then consigned to Tom to see delivered safely. Between whiles he and Tom were deep in murmured conversation.

All the time the noise and foetid air of Alsatia bored into Kate's consciousness until at last she was so accustomed to them that she was scarcely aware of them any more. By night a thick yellow fog would rise from the river and envelop the alley and all the area, and Blood forbade her to leave the house. 'Murder could be done, and often is, in this choking vapour, and none would know,' he told her.

After a week or two, Kate began to grow

203

impatient. There was little for her to do and she was forbidden to wander far from the sleazy little house. Tom had pointed out to her the steps towards the west which led up to Temple Gardens and had told her she was never to go beyond this point. Inside the house Kate could only go into her chamber or the little parlour where they ate; the rest of the house was for the whores only. Consequently she spent much of her time when Tom was busy in wandering the streets, the mass of narrow little alleys and lanes that made up Alsatia.

There was always plenty to be seen. Street brawls broke out frequently between traders and their customers, or whores wrangling over a client. Most of the buildings were small taverns where card-playing and shouting and fighting seemed to be the main preoccupations of the people inside. And above all the din, babies' screams and the wailing of badly-played fiddles could constantly be heard, day and night. Life went on busily, whatever the hour, and Kate had no opportunity to be bored while she waited for Blood to move.

Spring was coming, but the warmer air of Alsatia seemed only to enhance the odour of the streets. Kate came back to the house one afternoon to find Blood, Tom and Bess deep in conversation in the parlour. Bess, chin in hands, leaned on the greasy table listening intently to Blood's words.

Blood glanced up when Kate entered. 'Ah, Kate, my dear, I was just telling Tom and Bess that at last I am ready to make my plans known. Very soon now we shall strike, and Kate, I promise you this shall be a feat which will go down in history.'

Kate took off her cloak and sat down. Bess was gazing at the Colonel thoughtfully.

'But where does Kate fit into your plan, Colonel?' she asked.

Blood rose and crossed to the window. When he turned to face them he was smiling broadly.

'Kate,' he announced casually, 'is to be my wife.'

FIFTEEN

Bess half-started from her chair, then sat down again, clicking her tongue impatiently. 'You are not serious, Colonel. You have a wife already,' she murmured, and then added as another thought crossed her mind, 'at least, your wife has not died, has she? I know she has been ailing long.'

Tom chuckled. 'The Colonel is not concerned with matrimonial ventures now, Bess. He merely means that for the purposes of his plan, Kate will act as his wife. Is that not so, Colonel?'

'To be sure,' Blood nodded. 'It may take some days yet before all is settled, but let it suffice that I have my other fellow conspirators here, hard by in Whitefriars. As they are not concerned with the part of the plan in which I shall need your services, Kate, I do not intend that you and they should meet. Thus if any of you are taken prisoner, if our plan should miscarry, there is little you can tell.'

'But tell us more,' Kate breathed excitedly. The atmosphere of tension was mounting in the little room and the air of suppressed anticipation was communicating itself rapidly from one to another of the plotters. 'What is the plan, Colonel?'

Blood drew himself upright and paused, with all the command of an actor, Kate noted, before replying. 'We are to rob His Majesty of his Crown Jewels,' he said briefly.

Kate heard Bess's gasp as she clapped her

hand to her mouth. Tom was smiling in wonder, but his look changed to one of frowning puzzlement.

'But Colonel,' he protested, 'it is not long since you declined to harm the King. How is it you now wish to rob him?'

'I do not understand you, Tom.'

'Some little time ago you led us to Battersea early one morning – Parrett and me and several others – and told us we were to fire on the King as he swam in the river with the Duke, his brother. Yet at the last moment as we lay hidden in the reeds at the river's edge, you bade us all creep silently away and leave the King unharmed. Why did you do so, if you plan to rob him now?'

The Colonel gazed into the air as he listened. 'You are right, Tom. I did just as you say. I planned to execute the King in retribution for all the crimes which have been committed against Ireland and the Dissenters in the name of his government.'

'Then why did you forbid us to shoot?'

'I hardly know,' the Colonel's voice breathed softly. 'I had every intention of watching him die, yet as I saw him rise from the water I was overcome by his strength, his majesty. He has a broad, prepossessing brow, and an air of restrained strength, you know, Tom. I felt I detected a brotherly spirit and I could not harm him.'

Blood's air of introspection vanished suddenly. 'But to business, my friends. The plan now is to steal the Crown Jewels from the Tower. Their value is phenomenal, I am told, and we shall all be rich once the plan is carried out.'

Bess was still hunched over the table, wide-eyed. 'How do you mean to enter the Tower, for it is heavily guarded? Indeed, the troops garrisoned there make your plan sound impossible, Colonel.'

Blood laughed shortly. 'Naught is impossible, Bess, if one sets one's mind to it. And I have a scheme which is almost devilish in its cunning simplicity. Later you shall know all. For now, I will tell you that I am Dr Ayliffe, a country parson, and Kate is my gentle child-wife.'

Despite pressure from Bess and Kate, Blood would say no more. 'Tomorrow you shall go with Bess to a dressmaker, and for the Lord's sake, I implore you to order only the sober gown and cloak a parson's wife would wear. None of your silks and satins and tawdry lace – those you may order to your heart's content once we are all rich and safely far away from here.'

'And am I to order naught for myself?' Bess asked imperturbably, her hand jauntily braced on a jutting hip.

'I had forgot, Bess, to be sure you may. Order a fine sarcenet or moire gown, what you will, as a gift from me for your loyalty,' Blood answered with a smile. Bess's stiff manner softened instantly, and she began making arrangements with Kate for the morrow with an eager air that Kate had not seen hitherto.

In the morning Bess was waiting for her, having already eaten. She could scarcely be patient while Kate ate some rather dry meat pasty that Mistress Millichope brought her, but paced anxiously up and down the little parlour.

'Come, let us be gone,' she said at length when Kate had drunk her glass of ale, and the two girls hastened away through the crowded alleys of Whitefriars. In the dressmaker's little workshop Bess sighed ecstatically over the tiny manikins dressed in silks and worsteds, and deliberated far longer than Kate over what she would choose. The fine cream sarcenet undergown and gleaming rich red satin she eventually decided upon caused Kate a pang of envy, for she could order only what the Colonel had bidden her – a dark russet worsted gown with a trimming of solidly respectable lace. Nor could she order the provocatively low decolletage that Bess triumphantly pointed out to the quietly respectful little dressmaker. Ah well, thought Kate with resignation, my turn will come once all this secrecy is over.

As they walked homeward Bess was in high good humour, her eyes dancing with anticipation as she thought of her new gown. She was, apparently, even prepared to be friendly towards Kate.

'See there,' she said as they walked near the river bank, 'across the river there you can see the Tower, where our fortunes are to be made.'

Kate's eyes followed Bess's pointing finger. On the further bank of the river a huge grey battlemented building loomed dark and forbidding above the rest of the buildings clustered about it. Kate caught her breath. Somehow she had visualised the Tower Tom and Blood had spoken about as a tall, slender white tower like one heard of in fairy tales, but this monstrous edifice with its turrets and gates and battlements looked more like a castle, a fortress! How on earth, she wondered, would a handful of men breach the defences of a building such as this?

Bess was prattling on about the Tower and the garrison of troops quartered there, the arms and ammunition deposited there, and of the unfortunate queens and nobles accused of treason who had ended their days there. The more she told Kate of the place, the more Kate wondered at Colonel Blood's daring. Only a man of immense courage – or a madman – could conceive a plan to break into the defences of a place as impregnable as this.

She gave up wondering. It was useless to puzzle over Blood's intentions, she had learnt. None but he would ever know the full extent of his plans or his reasons. Like Tom and Bess she could only trust and obey.

The days could not pass quickly enough for Kate, for now she knew the plan was imminent she was anxious to begin and have it done with. What part she was to play as the Reverend Dr Ayliffe's wife she had yet to learn, and she wished Blood would tell her quickly so that she might begin to rehearse.

She did not have long to wait and wonder. After a week the dressmaker delivered the gowns and Bess was overjoyed at her elegant new appearance. She pranced and pirouetted up and down to let Kate have a covetous look at her crimson gown.

'Am I not as fine as the Queen?' Bess asked joyfully. 'Will I not catch every man's eye tonight?'

Kate thought of the lecherous leers she had glimpsed while passing through the hallway of Mistress Millichope's establishment, the greedy, grasping and lascivious chuckles as newly-arrived clients lurched drunkenly after some slatternly trollop, and she reflected that Bess had no need of further enhancement. Poor Bess. Perchance when this affair was over she would have money enough to be able to leave off her wretched way of life.

Kate surveyed herself in the cracked looking glass in her chamber with no such jubilation as Bess. True, she looked respectable and modestly well off in her new worsted gown, but its drab colour did little for her attractions. But for her red-gold hair, she thought, the picture she presented would have been a drab and dreary one indeed. The warm serge cloak, the hat and gloves which had also been delivered she considered dull, too. Ah well, at least the

Colonel would no doubt be pleased at the modest, retiring, unimpressive effect of her costume. She asked Bess where he was.

'In his chamber, I believe, or mayhap with Tom.'

Blood was not with Tom, nor was there any answer when Kate knocked at Tom's door. She turned the knob and peered in. By the little latticed window an elderly gentleman dressed in sombre black, unrelieved but for the silver buckles on his shoes, sat reading a little book, peering hard in the fast fading daylight. He craned his head round to look up curiously at Kate.

'I – I – beg your pardon, sir,' Kate stuttered in embarrassment. 'I fear I must have mistaken the room, for I sought Mr Hunt.'

'He is not here, my child,' the old man said in a cracked treble. 'But you are welcome to join me if you seek company. I am but reading from my breviary.'

'Thank you, you are kind, but I would not trouble you, sir,' Kate said, stepping back to close the door, and as she did she heard Blood's full-throated roar of amusement. The old man stood up from his stool and strode towards her.

'I think my disguise is effective enough,

Tom, for it has cozened our little Kate,' he called, still laughing heartily. Tom appeared from nowhere behind her and caught her waist in his strong arm. He too was laughing. Kate looked from one man to the other in disbelief.

'You did not recognise the Colonel, Kate, dressed as he is as the reverend gentleman, your husband,' Tom said, his eyes still dancing with good humour. 'Excellent, Colonel, as ever. No one has ever yet pierced any one of your many disguises, and your sleight of hand with the periwig and the paintbrush is not failing yet.'

There was no doubting his open admiration of his leader. Kate too was overcome with the subtlety of Blood's disguise, far more cunning than any she had ever seen on stage. The wide-skirted coat of his black suit and the wide-brimmed hat, bare of any lace or trimming, were perfect for a clergyman. Even his stoop-shouldered stance and his screwed-up eyes were exactly those of an elderly scholar. She, like Tom, was full of admiration.

Blood was regarding her with the same look of approval. 'Yes, indeed, with that rather innocent, bemused look you are wearing now, you are the perfect country parson's wife bewildered at the pace of London life. You will suit me perfectly, Kate.'

Tom beamed with pride on hearing her praised thus. 'I know she will act the part to perfection, Colonel, but you must teach her her lines first so she may rehearse,' he said, his arm still about her waist.

The Colonel shook his head. 'No lines, no speaking,' he said tersely. 'I fear your soft Irish voice would undo us, Kate, so I must insist that you do not speak, or at least only in a whisper.'

Kate stared at him. 'Then what am I to do, sir?'

Blood looked at her hard. 'Yes, I think the time has come. Tom, call for food and ale to be sent up to us here, and we shall discuss the plan here in private.'

After the food and ale had been brought in by a shambling Mistress Millichope, growling and grumbling about her old legs and having other matters to attend to, Blood drew up a stool and sat forward facing Tom and Kate, who sat on the edge of the bed.

'You and I, Kate, will go as many other visitors to London do, to look over the Tower and see the Crown Jewels where they lie locked but open to view. No,' he added, as Kate opened her mouth to speak, 'we shall not attempt to steal them then, but we shall simply survey the field, as it were, and see how matters lie.'

He took a mouthful of food before continuing. 'Tom and I have already confirmed that the jewels are kept in the Martin Tower and above the chamber are the apartments where live the Keeper and his wife and daughter. Edwards, the Keeper, is an elderly fellow, we are told, but I know not till I see him how hearty an opponent he may be. His son, who could well have been a hindrance to us, is fortunately away in the wars, in Holland I understand, and so we are blessed by his absence.'

Tom was nodding and listening thoughtfully. He did not attempt to speak when Blood paused, so Kate kept silent too. Eventually the Colonel went on.

'Your part in this affair, Kate, is simply to follow the visitors around with me dutifully. Then when we reach the Jewel Chamber I want you to become ill – faint, have a fit of the vapours or megrim, what you will – so long as you are so badly indisposed that I may call on the Keeper to help me tend you. With luck he will kindly offer the ministrations of his wife and thus we may be allowed to enter their private apartments.'

'But why, Colonel? There are no jewels up there, you said so yourself.' This time Kate could not keep her tongue still. Blood looked at her fondly.

'Indeed, that is so, little one. But as I said, I do not plan to attempt the theft yet. All I wish is to inveigle myself into the good graces of the family, to size up the situation. If Mistress Edwards has a care to your illness and is concerned for you, it will present me with the opportunity of returning later to thank them, to become more friendly with them, and who knows, perchance to work on them to aid me in my plan.'

He had that far-away look in his eyes again. Kate prompted him to carry on with his explanation. 'And Tom – is he to accompany us, Colonel?'

'Lord no! Tom is to be a chief actor in a later scene of the drama. For the first act it is to be only you and I, my dear.' Blood patted her shoulder and rose to go. He shambled across the floor and fumbled for the knob of the door, peering short-sightedly, and shuffled out, every inch the aged scholar. Tom laughed with delight.

'Is he not marvellous, Kate? Do you not

admire and love him as I do?'

'Admire him, yes,' Kate admitted, 'but love him? I know not. It would be hard to trust such a clever, scheming fellow enough to love him.'

'I love him,' Tom said stoutly, and looked away.

'Mayhap I shall also in time, but not yet,' Kate said quietly.

'Shall we go out for a walk?' Kate knew he was changing the subject deliberately, but she accepted quickly. It was not often now that she had the opportunity of being alone with Tom.

They walked in companionable silence for some time, the warmth of his hand reassuring on her arm. It was a mellow, pleasant evening but for the screeching and howling that always filled these narrow streets. By the river bank Tom paused and took her hand in his. By the dim light she could see the gleam of his bloodstone ring.

'What are you thinking of, Kate?' he asked her softly. 'Of the Colonel and his plan? Are you frightened, Kate?'

'No, no,' Kate hastened to say proudly. 'I am not afraid. If you trust Blood then so do I, wholeheartedly.'

'Then where were your thoughts, Kate, for

you were far away?'

Kate felt suddenly shy but she spoke proudly. 'I was remembering once, long ago it seems, in Ireland when an old gipsy foretold my fortune.'

'And what did she tell you, Kate? Did it come true?' His voice was gentle but vibrant in the darkness, and Kate trembled involuntarily.

'Some of what she told me did indeed come to pass. Fire and death, and crossing the water. And a man with a bloodstone who would change my life. A man of courage.' Kate said the last words in a voice so low that Tom had to bend closer to hear her.

'Courage?' Tom repeated. 'That was the Colonel.'

'But the bloodstone is yours.'

'And you think I will change your life, Kate? More like it is the Colonel, for his plan will soon make you rich.'

'I care naught for riches!' Kate retorted, her pride stung, and instantly she regretted her words. Tom was no fool. No doubt he would read her meaning, that she would prefer Tom to change her life than the Colonel and his plans. She hung her head with embarrassment. Tom lifted her chin gently with his finger.

'The Colonel would tell you that all this fortune-telling is mere flummery, Kate,' he said quietly. 'He would tell you, as he has often told me, that there is no such thing as destiny. Life is what we ourselves make of it.'

'And what has he made of his life?' Kate demanded angrily. 'He is still a criminal, a wanted man with a price on his head, hunted and homeless. Can he claim to have made a life that is worth living?'

'He does as his conscience dictates and that is the best that any of us can do,' Tom answered quietly. 'Homeless perchance, but never friendless. The Colonel is one of the most admired men in the country. And mayhap when he has finished he will be wealthy too. If he is not, then it will not be for the want of trying.'

Kate snorted. Sometimes she felt that Tom carried his hero-worship of this man too far. Blood was clever and likeable, yes, but he was no idol to be adored so openly.

Then Kate realised that her resentment of Tom's admiration was probably because she was jealous. She would have liked Tom to glow so enthusiastically about her instead of about Blood. He seemed to like her well enough, indeed he sought her company and never Bess's. And as they walked homeward his fingers pressed warmly on her gloved hand.

At the doorway he kissed her, briefly but with an urgency that thrilled Kate. She could have cursed aloud when Blood appeared in the doorway.

'Come,' he said tersely. 'There are matters to discuss. Tomorrow we go to the Tower.'

SIXTEEN

Old Talbot Edwards walked down the stone stairs of the Martin Tower with some difficulty. His old bones no longer took kindly to the cold and the damp of the clammy old building, and he was glad to emerge at last into the warm spring sunlight outside.

Troopers enjoying the sunshine loitered around, interspersed with citizens who were seeking amusement. Old Edwards smiled happily. There would be a fair sprinkling of visitors to see the Crown Jewels today, and a fair proportion of the fees for himself once he had handed over a share to the Master of the Jewel House, Sir Gilbert. Fortunately Sir Gilbert spent most of his time at court in Whitehall, and consequently he had no check as to how many visitors passed through the Martin Tower. Yes, it was an enviable post, to be Deputy Keeper of the Jewels, Edwards thought once again contentedly.

Light footsteps crossed the greensward towards him. Edwards screwed up his eyes against the sunlight and recognised the fair, pretty face of his daughter.

'Annis,' he said severely, 'where have you been? Not gossiping with the troopers again, I trust? I have told you I did not wish you to mingle with rough creatures like them.'

'Oh Father!' The girl's gentle voice was edged with impatience. 'You are constantly telling me I am of an age where I should be married and bearing children, yet you will not let me speak with a man. How else am I to meet a husband, confined as I am in the Tower like poor Queen Anne?'

Edwards' voice was testy, for he resented being continually reminded by his daughter that she dwelt where Anne Boleyn had died cruelly by the headsman's axe. 'Men there are a-plenty, mistress, but none here suitable for a husband for you. And you the Deputy Keeper's daughter! I want no common trooper for a son-in-law.'

'Only a son,' Annis replied mischievously. Edwards turned away impatiently, reluctant to speak sharply to the beloved child of his old age. Moreover he did not want her to see how his heart was saddened by the reference to his son, far away in Holland.

If only he could find some means to discover a husband for Annis. A gentleman preferably, but in any event a sober, respectable man, none of your philandering soldiers who sought only the lights of love for their passing amusement. He had been hard put to it to keep the girl out of their reach but she would keep disobeying him. Luckily, he knew, she had no intention of doing more than pass the time with them, for she was perpetually bored, as she frequently told both him and her mother. Occasionally he would allow her to walk along the wharf to gain some air, but the language and behaviour of the wherrymen was really far too shocking for a maid of Annis's sheltered upbringing. Oh, if only he could find a husband for her, to shed this burden of worry from his mind! But the maid was turned twenty now, and unless he found a suitable match for her very soon, she would be doomed to spinsterhood, poor wench!

'Pardon me sir.' Edwards was jerked out of his mood of self-pity by a gentle voice at his elbow. He turned as sharply as his rheumaticky legs would allow, and saw a venerable gentleman, soberly dressed in black, regarding him with an air of bewilderment. Behind him stood a pretty young maid with bright red hair escaping from under her hat and gleaming brilliantly in the April sunlight.

'At your service, sir,' Edwards said to the gentleman, for such he evidently was. A civil word or two would not go amiss, and might even earn him an extra fee.

The old gentleman gazed at him with confusion in his dark eyes. 'I regret to trouble you, sir, but you appear to be a gentleman of some importance hereabouts, and I seem to have lost my way.'

Edwards was touched by the old man's courtesy, and he was obviously well-bred to be able to recognise the importance of the Deputy Keeper. He drew himself up to his full height, as in his old soldiering days.

'Let me help you, sir,' he said in his most

agreeable manner.

'I sought the Jewel House, to show the Crown Jewels to my young wife here,' the old man said, twisting and gazing about him in obvious bewilderment. Edwards was mildly surprised that a lady so young could be the old man's wife; his daughter he would have believed, but there was no accounting for folk's ways. 'You see, I came here once in my youth, many years ago, and I distinctly remembered the Jewel House as lying to the east of the White Tower,' the old man went on, 'but now I can find naught here but an old ruined derelict. It is most confusing.'

Edwards smiled tolerantly. 'That was indeed a long time ago sir, for the jewels have lain this many a year in the jewel room in the Martin Tower. I, sir, am the keeper, and I would be honoured to show the jewels to you and your good lady.'

It was early yet and no other visitors were in sight, so he could afford to patronise the fussy old man. The gentleman was agreeably surprised and impressed by his kindness.

'I am most grateful to you, sir, for I had promised my wife and would have been most unhappy to disappoint her – in her present condition,' he murmured in an undertone as they turned to cross the grass towards the Martin Tower. Edwards snorted. No doubt the old man thought himself very clever to be still able to father a child, and was anxious to let everyone know about his cleverness. Still, he himself was nearly sixty when he sired Annis, and he remembered yet the pride he had felt at his achievement.

The gentleman shuffled along beside him, chatting about how pleased he was to have met the Deputy Keeper himself. He was a parson, he said, in the depths of the country, and was anxious to bring his new, young wife to see the sights London had to offer. The young wife in question walked quietly along behind them, her hands folded and a demure expression on her young face. A dutiful young wife, Edwards thought approvingly. Now if Annis could behave as submissively as that, instead of being impetuous and mischievous, perhaps she too could catch the eye of a respectable man like the Reverend.

He entered the gloom of the Martin Tower and his guests followed him eagerly. Ascending the steps to the Jewel Room, Edwards saw the Reverend considerately take his wife's arm to help her. She looked pale and wan. Edwards felt a trifle sorry for the weak, silent creature.

'Tell me, mistress, does this place affright you? It is said the ghost of Anne Boleyn walks at night though I've seen and heard naught myself.'

He stood in the centre of the room and awaited her reply. The lady darted a questioning look at her husband, and then looked meekly towards the floor. Her husband took it upon himself to reply.

'I regret my wife is somewhat shy, sir, but she is as excited as I at the prospect of seeing the regalia. It is kept here now you say?' The old man peered eagerly about him. The lady stood by the steps. Perchance she had been dazzled by the sun and was having difficulty in adjusting to the gloom. Edwards closed the door behind them and slid the bolt home. The lady gasped.

'Excuse me, mistress, but it is my custom always to lock the door,' Edwards explained gruffly. Whatever her condition, he could make no exception in her case. She would have to endure the closeness and gloom for a few moments.

He crossed to the further wall, where a ray of sunlight from the high, barred window illuminated a somewhat dusty curtain across a recess. He drew back the curtain with a flourish, revealing the contents of the barred recess with pride, and awaited his audience's reaction.

Their gasps were rewardingly gratifying. The sun flashed brilliantly and rebounded from the golden crown, orb and sceptre which lay magnificently couched on purple velvet, surrounded by all the lesser treasures of state, staffs and salt cellars and gilded crests. Jewels blazed from every piece, their iridescent colours flashing in the sunlight.

The old reverend advanced slowly towards them, his dark eyes alive with eager curiosity. 'Magnificent! Breathtaking!' he murmured as if to himself. 'The very symbols of majesty, wife, are they not wonderful? See, here is the golden ampulla and the spoon used to anoint the King, of solid gold both. Oh, Mr Edwards, what a responsibility you carry, to be warden of such treasure as this!'

Edwards preened himself. 'To be sure it is a responsible task, sir, but I am proud of the honour. The crown cost eight thousand pounds and the orb eleven hundred, not to mention the value of all these emeralds and sapphires. That is why the recess is so securely barred.'

'And is it never opened?' the old man enquired.

Edwards hesitated. 'Very rarely, sir. And only when I decide, for I am the only man to hold the keys to it.'

The reverend shook his head wonderingly. The lady uttered a sound like a faint sigh, and Edwards saw her husband look at her and then frown.

'Are you not well, my love?' he asked tenderly. The lady shook her head slowly. 'I fear Mistress Ayliffe perchance feels the lack of air in here,' the gentleman said to Edwards. 'Much as I regret to leave the sight of so much wonder, I think it were best you unlocked the door and let me take my wife to the air.'

He sighed reflectively and took a last, lingering look at the jewels. Edwards crossed to draw the curtain over them, irritated by this cutting short of his moment of glory. As his hand touched the curtain he heard a faint moan and a rustle.

'Oh, my wife! She has fainted!' the old man cried, and rushed to where the young woman lay inert on the stone steps. He began fanning her face and rubbing her hands, calling to her, but she did not move.

The reverend looked up at Edwards with bewildered eyes. 'What am I to do? Help me, sir, I beseech you, for I am helpless in these matters!'

Edwards unlocked the door and called up the stairs to his wife. In seconds Mistress Edwards and Annis came running.

'What is amiss, husband?' His wife gaped blankly at him, but Annis took in the situation quickly.

'There is a lady here in a swoon, mother. Let us get her upstairs and revive her.'

'What ails her, sir?' Mistress Edwards asked the reverend. 'A fit of the vapours, perchance, or an attack of the colic?'

'Cease your fussing, woman,' said Edwards in his curtest military manner. 'Can you not see the lady is in a delicate condition and must be attended to on the instant? There is no time for clacking.'

He locked the door of the chamber firmly, then between them they managed to carry the young lady upstairs, where they laid her comfortably on a sofa. She lay white and motionless for some time, and Edwards began to think the old reverend would have an attack of apoplexy soon, so much he fussed over her.

Eventually the girl's eyes opened. Annis

brought brandy and the girl sipped it weakly, then closed her eyes and shook her head.

'No more,' she sighed in a whisper. 'I am well now.'

'The Lord be praised!' the reverend ejaculated, clasping his hands in prayer. The young woman smiled at him fondly.

Edwards was more than gratified by the old gentleman's rapturous thanks for his help and prompt action. 'And to Mistress Edwards and your pretty young daughter here I must convey my deepest gratitude,' he smiled happily, 'for what would my poor wife have done without you? But we can trouble you no longer, Mr Edwards, and if you would be kind enough to call a hackney for us, I will take my wife home.'

'Not at all!' Mistress Edwards intervened. 'A lady in her condition should rest some time yet before she can be moved, or who knows what harm may befall! When is the child expected, may I ask?'

The lady's eyelids fluttered shyly downwards.

'In October, we understand,' the reverend answered her. Edwards could see his wife's gaze on the ceiling as she made rapid calculations.

'Then it is indeed a dangerous time,' she concluded at last. 'It would be wiser far to let the lady rest some hours here, to ensure that no harm has been done, before you move her. My husband and I would be delighted to have you stay to dinner with us.'

'Madam, you are too kind.' The reverend bowed somewhat stiffly. 'But in view of my concern for my wife's safety, I will accept your generous offer.'

Edwards grunted. 'Well, if you will excuse me, sir, I have work to attend to below,' he pointed out. 'Other visitors will be waiting.'

'Of course, of course, do not let our little mishap distract you from your very important tasks,' the old man said genially. 'I am most indebted to you and your family, and if I may be allowed, I should like to call on you again some day soon.'

'Delighted to see you,' said Edwards curtly. 'Now I must be gone.'

He descended the stone stairs again, rather more stiffly than before. What a to-do, what a fuss about a wench with child having a swoon! His back, still aching with the effort of helping to carry her, would remind him of the event for days if not weeks to come, drat it! And he had not secured the fee, much less an extra emolument from the old gentleman after all.

It caused a slight flicker of amusement and a few momentarily raised eyebrows that night among Mistress Millichope's clients, to see a pretty but plainly-dressed girl accompanied by an aged parson entering the bawdy house. Once inside the haven of Mistress Millichope's parlour, however the parson and the maid were both convulsed with noisy laughter.

Tom and Bess sat by the low fire. Tom rose eagerly to meet them, but Kate could only sit with tear-filled eyes, rocking to and fro, choking with laughter.

'Well? How did it go?' Tom demanded.

'Yes, tell us quickly,' Bess urged, but Blood only stood, his elbow leaning on the mantelshelf, and roared as noisily as Kate.

'Kate, you were the sweetest, most simpering little goosebrain it has ever been my pleasure to meet,' Blood gasped at last, wiping the tears from his cheeks. 'You were perfect, by my troth!'

'And you the fussiest, most short-sighted doddering old parson!' shrieked Kate, relapsing again into fits of giggles. 'I swear, Colonel, you would do credit to any troupe of actors! Such a convincing old cretin I have never seen!'

Blood tapped his forehead significantly. 'But I am not so crazy as I seemed, Kate. Today I discovered all that I needed to know to complete my plan.'

'Tell us, sir,' Tom interrupted. 'Tell us what you found out. Bess and I have been dying of curiosity all day to know how you both fared.'

'It went just as we had planned it, Tom. I looked every inch the parson, thanks to the sober suit you procured me, Bess, clever girl. And Kate fainted nobly as she was ordered. The result was, we were invited in to rest and sup and now there is little I do not know about old Edwards' habits, thanks to his chatterbox wife. But ring for some ale, Bess my lass, for my throat burns like the very pit of hell from all that laughing.'

Kate's paroxysms of laughter had ceased by now and she listened as intently as the other two to the Colonel's graphic account of the day's adventure. He had a way with him and no mistake, holding his audience spellbound as he spoke.

'And Edwards himself is the only man with a key both to the Jewel Chamber and to the barred gate across the recess, I find,'

Blood concluded. 'Hence it is imperative we cozen the old man to open up for us of his own free will. To this end I must pursue his friendship further.'

'But how may you do that, Colonel?' Bess asked.

'You, my Bess, must buy me six of the finest pairs of gloves you can find – silk, embroidered, perfumed, or what you will.'

'Gloves?' Bess repeated, puzzled. 'Why gloves?'

'Because I heard Mistress Edwards say she had a passion for gloves, my beauty, and what could be more natural than that I should call to thank her for her kindness, making her a small present as a token of my gratitude?'

'But what then, sir?' Tom enquired. 'There must be some plan in your mind as to how you will follow up this strategy?'

'There is indeed, Tom. It was a pity you were not with us today, my boy, for you would have seen and appreciated one of the bonniest prisoners that odious Tower can ever have confined. Edwards' daughter, I mean, a fair and lively lass of about your own age.'

'And what of her?' Tom's voice was mildly curious.

'What of her? What complete lack of concern you display, my lad, for the maid whom you are to begin courting.' Blood feigned astonishment.

'Courting?' Tom and Kate uttered the word in unison. Blood smiled his secret, mischievous smile again.

'Aye, why not? The old couple are anxious to find a gentleman suitable for their little maid, as the old lady made clear. I doubt not they would be delighted to have the parson's nephew come paying his attentions to her, so think on it, boy. Rehearse your pretty compliments and gallant ways for when Bess has the gloves and I return to the Tower, I shall mention casually to the Edwards that I have a nephew who is endowed both with a handsome appearance and a comfortable income.'

Tom laughed, and Bess began teasing him, but Kate did not join in the merriment. She had seen for herself how dainty as porcelain and fair Annis Edwards was, and Tom was as human as any man. She burned inwardly with jealousy.

SEVENTEEN

Some days passed before Blood set off, once again in his sober clergyman's suit, to the Tower. This time he took with him the six pairs of silk gloves that Bess had bought at his request.

At nightfall he returned, highly pleased with his day's achievements. Mr Edwards had been gruffly pleased and Mistress Edwards flutteringly delighted at his unexpected call and he had been invited to stay and sup with them again. By evening they had received a fulsome account of the Reverend Dr Ayliffe's charming nephew, rich but retiring by nature, and of the reverend's desire to get the young man safely married and settled down.

'And did they rise to the bait, Colonel?' Tom asked eagerly.

'Like any stupid fish,' Blood replied happily. 'They told me of their similar problem over Annis and from there it was not a long step to their suggesting, diffidently, but oh, so earnestly, that the young

237

couple should meet. It was their idea, Tom lad; I did naught but raise my eyebrows in pleased surprise and congratulate them on their clever idea.'

'What next then, Colonel?' Bess leaned her elbows on her knees, cradling her chin in her hands.

'Yes, when do we meet?' Tom urged.

'Not so fast, lad! You're as anxious a swain as ever any village lad was! We must not appear over-anxious, so I told them it would be some days before you would be free to call.'

Kate kept silent during this exchange. She still felt a curious stab of jealousy and distrust at the thought of Tom and Annis together. At the same time she was eager for Blood's plan to be over and done, so they could leave this loathsome, vile-smelling part of London far behind them.

'They enquired after your health, Kate, and I told them you were resting carefully now, and Mistress Edwards sends you a dozen recipes for restoratives and tonics I cannot now recall,' Blood went on. 'They are obviously very well-disposed towards our family, and Tom will be received there open-armed, I know it.'

'By the wench also?' Tom said with a grin.

Blood rubbed his chin thoughtfully. 'No, not by Mistress Annis, I fancy, for she tossed a stubborn head whenever your name was mentioned. So it will be for you, my dashing gallant, to soften her heart and win her over with your charming ways.'

Kate turned to look out of the window. She did not want the others to see the angry flush that reddened her cheeks.

'What is there for Bess and me to do now?' she asked quietly. No mention had been made of any further action for them.

'Naught, my lovelies, but bide here patiently and be ready at all times for us. Once we have the jewels we shall lie low here for a few days, and then fly. Where shall it be, Kate? To our lush and lovely Ireland, eh?'

He caught her hands and spun her round. Kate felt he had sensed her mood and was endeavouring to cajole her out of it.

'Shall it be Ireland, Kate? Or Holland? Or France? Wherever it is, we shall have time and wealth then to disport ourselves as we please. You may enjoy Tom's company to the full, and I my sweet Bess's, eh Bess?'

He dropped Kate's hands and turned to grab Bess, but she ducked and eluded him, giggling as she ran.

A few days later Kate and Bess watched through the latticed window as Blood and Tom set off together to the Tower. Kate thought she had never seen Tom look as handsome as he did at this moment, in his lace-trimmed peacock blue suit and his velvet-lined cloak. He was a visitor to stir any maiden's youthful heart. She turned restlessly away from the window when the two men reached the corner of the alley.

'Come, Bess, let us amuse ourselves,' she said drily, but the words stuck in her throat. She had no wish to be amused, saddened as she was by Tom's absence and his proximity to that pretty little wheyfaced Edwards chit. The day dragged along wearily for Kate until nightfall. Every clatter of a footstep outside the house made her sit up hopefully, but often it was only a client for one of Mistress Millichope's wenches.

At last she heard steps on the stairs that she recognised. With great effort Kate managed to make herself sit still and not run to meet them, and she smiled with relief when Blood strode in, closely followed by Tom.

'Ah, that was a job well done,' sighed Blood, tossing his cloak aside and sinking into a chair. 'What say you, Tom? I think we have the fish hooked, would you not agree?'

Tom grinned contentedly. 'I think so, Colonel. Even the fair maiden unbent so far as to speak kindly to me by this evening. She's a pretty maid, is she not?'

'You liked her then?' Bess asked, pouring out liberal helpings of ale into tankards for them both.

'She liked *him* more than somewhat, and that is more to the point!' the Colonel exploded. 'She was besotted with him, any man with half an eye could see that, and old Edwards was delighted, I can tell you. I'm to go again to see about drawing up a marriage contract. How is that for progress in a day?'

Kate kept her face averted. Of course she was pleased that the Colonel's plan was working out so well, but the pleasure was marred by this ridiculous feeling of jealousy. So Tom had commented on the girl's beauty, but what of that? It did not necessarily indicate that he was smitten by her.

In any event, he could not pursue any lasting relationship with this Annis creature, or the Colonel's plan would be quite undone. Kate drew what consolation she could from the thought.

Later that evening, Blood went to see his other fellow-plotters, Tom asked Kate if she would like to take a walk by the river bank. Torch lights across the river twinkled on the surface of the water, and Tom walked alongside Kate in silence. At length he paused and turned to face her.

'Kate, there is a matter I have long wanted to talk of with you, but the time is not ripe.'

He paused and looked at her uncertainly. 'Yes?' Kate prompted him, her heart fluttering at his probing look.

'Kate, I am a soldier, and I follow the Colonel wherever he may lead me. At a time like this we are virtually at war, and while I am concerned in a campaign, I can devote my mind to no other matter.'

'A person of single-minded purpose, I see,' Kate murmured, keeping her eyes on the river.

'You do not see! Oh Kate, how can I explain to you? This venture of the Colonel's is the most important plan we have ever attempted, and at the same time the most dangerous. If we slip, Kate, if we are caught – you know the penalty for treason.'

Kate shuddered at the implication of his words. She knew only too well the penalty, and her vivid imagination tried to repulse a sudden, horrible vision of Tom dangling, neck awry, at the end of a rope.

Tom sauntered on, kicking idly at a stone as he considered his words.

'Let me tell you only that I care about you, Kate, and I am saddened to see how dispirited you seem of late. Kate, you are not feeling remorseful over your husband, are you?'

Kate realised with a start that she had given Val scarcely a moment's thought since she wept her last tear for him. 'No, of course not,' she said quietly.

'Then what is it?'

'I am concerned for you, that is all.'

Tom laughed. 'Is that all? Then have no fear, for the Colonel and I have escaped many a worse situation than this. We may be surrounded by troopers once we enter the Tower, but we shall emerge unscathed, I promise you. Blood has the luck of the devil, and like a cat, he has not yet used up all of his nine lives.'

He took Kate by the shoulders. She could not tell him that he had mistaken her concern for him, so she let matters be. Tom was regarding her seriously.

'Smile again, Kate, for the sun is hidden

behind cloud when you are sad. When all this is over, I shall make you happy again. Only wait for me, won't you?'

She smiled up at him, full of happiness. 'I shall always wait for you, Tom,' she said. He kissed her very gently, and then led her home.

Blood was waiting for them at the inn. 'Parrett and Holloway are preparing, Tom. They know their parts and will be ready for us. Away to your bed now, for we must be up betimes in the morning.'

On the landing they separated, and Kate stood alone, forgotten for the moment, but perfectly content at heart.

It was early light when Blood awoke Tom and bade him prepare. Tom, as he had anticipated, rubbed his eyes and complained that it was still far too early to go a-visiting.

'Not at all, lad,' Blood rumbled. 'If we take them unawares, the more chance there is we may get to the jewels.'

Tom did not question his reasoning, but did as he was bidden. They went on foot, and although it was still early many people were already abroad, preparing for their day's work. Outside the Tower Blood pointed to the spot where Holloway would be waiting with the horses. Parrett was awaiting them at the gate, his sandy hair bristling under his plumed hat and his hollow face alight with anticipation.

'Now you know your part, Parrett,' Blood reminded him. 'You are my legal friend who is to draw up the marriage contract, but fear not, we shall not stretch your legal brain, for we shall tackle our other business before we reach that point. You have a pistol, and a rapier concealed in your cane as I bade you?'

'Aye, Colonel,' Parrett replied eagerly, and would have withdrawn the blade to prove it if Blood had not stayed his hand.

'That is good. Hunt has a file and I the mallet, so all is provided for. Now let us approach.'

Soldiers were already at work, drilling stiffly on the green in the dawn light. Blood walked confidently up to the Martin Tower and rang the bell. When no answer came immediately he rang again, loudly and imperiously. After some moments a dishevelled Edwards appeared.

'What in the name of Heaven...?' he began irritably, but cut himself short when he recognised Blood. 'Oh sir, it is you! I had not expected you so early,' he stammered.

Blood looked surprised.

'Not expecting us, Mr Edwards?' he repeated in apparent amazement. 'But I told you I would come again with my nephew and a legal friend this morning.'

'This morning, so you did, sir, but I did not think you meant so early as seven,' Edwards murmured, obviously ill at ease and anxious not to upset his distinguished visitors. He smoothed down his wispy grey hair and adjusted his half-buttoned coat. 'I'm afraid my wife has only just risen and will not be ready to receive you yet, sir, not in the way a gentleman should be received, that is,' he added, hastening to rectify what might appear to be a discourteous rebuff.

'I am so sorry, Mr Edwards, I had no intention of putting you or your wife to any inconvenience,' Blood said hesitantly. 'But we can hardly retrace our steps so far. Can you perhaps suggest some way in which we might pass the time until your good lady and Mistress Annis are ready for us?'

Blood blinked short-sightedly into old Edwards' face, and then suddenly snapped his fingers as if a startling idea had just occurred to him.

'I have it! The Jewels! Mr Edwards, perhaps you would be so kind as to delight my nephew and my friend here with a glimpse of those magnificent treasures you guard so capably. I know they would be as entranced as Mistress Ayliffe and myself were at their beauty, would you not, gentlemen?'

Tom and Parrett nodded and agreed vigorously, and after only a moment's perceptible hesitation old Edwards grunted and turned to lead the way. Blood kept chattering amiably as they walked.

'My friends, you will see such a sight as will take your breath away, I assure you,' he gabbled, watching Edwards withdraw a cluster of keys from his pocket to unlock the oaken door with its iron hinges. 'We really are most indebted to you for your kindness, Mr Edwards.'

Edwards slid back the huge bolts and opened the door, motioning them to enter. The three men went in, and he followed, closing and locking the door carefully again on the inside.

As he did so, Tom raised his eyebrows in query to Blood, who shook his head firmly. He knew the lad was asking if this was the moment to strike Edwards down, but Blood was not ready yet. He had to ensure first that Edwards had the key to the grille where the treasure lay.

'Such sparkle, such brilliance you have never seen, my friends,' Blood began raving excitedly as Edwards padded across the stone-flagged floor to the recess and drew back the curtain. 'There!'

Tom and Parrett stood aghast at the sight of the crown, the orb and the sceptre reclining on their velvet cushion. Fortunately for Blood's purposes, the May morning was dull and the sunlight did not dance on the gems, enhancing their beauty as it had done on the last occasion.

'Oh, how sad!' he cried in disappointment. 'It is so gloomy in here and the sun is not shining, so we can hardly see them! If only we could take them out and look at them more closely!'

He looked sadly at Edwards, who remained impassive. 'But of course,' Blood continued, 'it is beyond your authority to touch them. Forgive me for suggesting it, my dear friend.'

Edwards was stung by the slight and Blood was delighted. 'It is not beyond my authority at all, Dr Ayliffe,' he said testily. 'In the absence of the Master I am in complete charge and indeed I am the only person with authority to unlock the grille.'

'Of course, forgive me, I fear I grow rather forgetful in my age,' Blood said soothingly.

'And indeed I have permitted certain people – a few, you understand, a favoured few – to hold them for a moment, but it is a very rare privilege.'

'To be sure, for members of the family only, as it were,' Blood murmured in agreement.

A silence hung between them. Blood purposely did not state what was implicit in his words – that Tom would very soon be son-in-law to Edwards and thus a member of his family. He could see by the thoughtful furrow on old Edwards' brow that the thought had germinated there. This, added to the fact that the old man was in a rather embarrassing position at the moment, having to keep his guests waiting, would soon decide the issue, Blood conjectured.

'Very well,' Edwards said at last with some reluctance. 'For you, Dr Ayliffe, I shall grant the privilege.' He fumbled in his pocket again for the keys, and Blood saw the eager light shine in Tom's eyes.

'Oh, Mr Edwards, I shall treasure this moment all my life,' Blood enthused in his high, cracked voice, and as Edwards unlocked the grille and swung it back, grating rustily on its hinges, Blood nodded to Tom over the old man's head.

Instantly Tom came to life. He leapt forward, swinging the cloak from his shoulders and throwing it over the old man's head. Edwards staggered and clutched at the cloak, grunting in surprise. From beneath the folds of his voluminous cloak Blood produced a mallet, and with it he hit Edwards hard on the head through the folds of Tom's cloak.

'Quick now, have you the gag, Tom? I have not hit him hard and he could recover before we are done.'

Tom produced a wooden plug tied to a length of cloth, and this he shoved into Edwards' mouth, tying the ends securely. Parrett meanwhile produced a length of rope with which he bound the old man tightly. Blood watched them working swiftly and silently, then turned his attention to the recess.

'I'll take the crown, and you, Tom, the sceptre. File it in half, the easier to dispose of it in your pockets. Parrett – take the orb.'

Parrett stuffed the ungainly item into a capacious pocket he had had specially made in his breeches, and its bulk was hidden by his cloak. Blood was having difficulty in stowing the crown under his cloak, so he withdrew it and gave it a few hefty blows with the mallet. Bent and distorted, he found he could then hide it adequately. Tom was panting with the effort of filing the sceptre in half, but at length he succeeded. He stuffed the pieces into his breeches, then looked about for his cloak. It still lay on the floor, covering the inert figure of Edwards. Tom bent to retrieve it. As he did so, Edwards moved and groaned.

'Keep silent, old man, or you'll undo us yet!' cried Parrett, and pulled out his dagger and jabbed the old man with it. Blood shouted furiously.

'Leave him be! I want the blood of no defenceless old man on my hands! Put away your dagger and let us be gone!'

He turned for the door and then remembered the keys. He hastened back to snatch them from where they still hung from the grille and then unlocked the door cautiously. At the very moment that he was withdrawing the bolt, a hearty voice just outside the door rang through the air.

'Mother! Father! I'm home! Where are you?'

Blood, Tom and Parrett gazed at each other mystified.

'What, no welcome for the hero home from the wars?' the jovial voice cried. 'Where is the soldier's welcome, the fatted calf for the prodigal son?'

Delighted shouts upstairs came to the ears of the men crouched in the Jewel Chamber below. 'Dear God, it's the old man's son!' Blood muttered. 'What are we to do now?' He kept his ear close to the door. 'He is going upstairs. In a moment we will run, boys. Holloway is waiting with horses at the gate.'

Tom and Parrett crouched close behind the Colonel. In a moment he nodded, then opened the door quietly and they all ran out. They raced across the parade ground, where the troopers were no longer drilling, and past the White Tower towards the drawbridge. None of the fortress's inhabitants, intent on their day's work, paid any attention to them until a voice, loud and strident, rang out across the sward.

'Stop! Treason! Stop thief! The Crown is stolen!'

Blood glanced over his shoulder as he ran. 'Young Edwards and the girl!' he gasped. 'And another soldier! Run for the gate!'

The pursuers were still far behind, but their cries of 'Treason' and 'Thief' awoke the dazed onlookers to action. Blood, Tom and Parrett pushed and thrust their way viciously through the pack who closed in on them, but their pace was slowed so much that young Edwards caught up with them.

'You take the older man, Beckman!' Edwards cried, and threw himself on Tom. Blood staggered and fell as the other soldier cannoned into him, and the two men rolled in the dust of the Tower yard. The gate was only two feet away, but Blood could not reach it. He drew out his pistol and fired, but he must have missed, for the soldier Beckman threw himself on Blood again.

The crown fell from Blood's pocket and rolled unevenly away, coming to rest in the dust. A soldier grabbed it up.

'Run, Tom, for God's sake,' Blood bawled, his mouth full of blood and dust, but from the corner of his vision as he scuffled with Beckman he saw Tom taken and pinioned fast, just beyond the gate. Voices around shrieked and yelled, but above them Blood heard horses' hooves clattering away at a gallop. With luck Parrett had got away with some of the booty.

Beckman threw himself on Blood again, and this time he sat so hard on Blood's chest that he was winded, and with extreme reluctance he was obliged to admit defeat. Of all the confounded luck! What a time for the Edwards youth to choose to return home, bringing a hefty soldier comrade with him! But for that ill-timed coincidence, his plan would have succeeded perfectly.

Blood rose, gasping, and let himself be led back towards the Tower. Tom staggered alongside him, dazed, and his eyes showing his sickened defeat. Oh well, thought Blood, so long as Parrett had got away, there was still hope that his friends might manage to contrive his escape. But Blood's optimism was to suffer another blow. As he stood inside the Tower, now silent and uncommunicative, more soldiers entered, leading Parrett who was trussed and bloodstreaked.

'He galloped off, but ran into a projecting pole, sir,' a soldier told the officer. 'Only the man who was holding the horses got away.'

Blood's heart sank. What was to have been his greatest achievement had come to naught after all. It was a bitter blow. He glanced at Beckman roguishly. 'Ah well,' he commented drily, 'it was at all events a stroke for a crown.'

Beckman grunted.

EIGHTEEN

Kate paced restlessly up and down the little parlour all morning, unable to settle herself to anything. For the first time she felt real fear for Tom and the Colonel's safety. How marvellous, how ambitious Blood's plan had seemed while they sat talking of it by candlelight at nights all these weeks, but now somehow the whole scheme seemed to have taken on a dizzy, hare-brained look.

It was because Tom and Blood were not by to fire her with their enthusiasm, she thought. Blood's zeal and eagerness had made the scheme tempting and noble, but alone Kate felt it was mad, foolish to the extreme. To think of it! Three men, and an accomplice waiting with horses, thought to tackle a whole garrisoned fortress! They could never do it! They would be captured and hanged, and what was there she could do to prevent it?

Kate was glad of Bess's company, though she too was repressed and silent today. Kate knew Bess cared deeply for Blood and the same thoughts that were tormenting Kate's mind were no doubt vexing hers. She sat listlessly in the window, watching along the alley.

Towards midday Mistress Millichope shuffled in. She pushed wisps of straying grey hair back under her greasy cap and beckoned Bess.

'Bess, come down a while, there's a merchant below who has drunk more than his fill and is asking for a pretty wench. Come down and talk to him, for he's money and to spare in his pocket.'

Bess sighed impatiently. 'Give him Nancy or one of the others, for I am occupied,' she snapped.

'I need you, Bess. With your looks and manner you could doubtless part him from his gold without even taking him to your bed. Come now, girl, it'll not take long if yer put yer mind to it.'

Mistress Millichope held the door open invitingly. Bess sighed wearily and rose, casting one final glance along the alley before she left.

Kate took Bess's seat at the window. The street was alive with crawling humanity and piercing noise, but of Tom and the Colonel there was no sign. How much longer would they be? They had been gone for five hours already. Kate grew more and more uneasy.

What a mad scheme it had been! What fools they had all been to listen to a crazed old man like Blood! But there was no doubt, the man had a kind of magnetism that inspired his listeners and made them all willing and eager to do his bidding. They had all gladly fallen under his spell.

But not any more, Kate determined fiercely. Once he and Tom came back she would free herself of this man's domination. If only she could persuade Tom to see him in his true colours too! What was it about Blood that had held Tom mesmerised all these years?

Kate's angry musings were cut short by Bess, bursting the door open and standing there, open-mouthed and panting. She was white with shock.

'Kate – they've been taken,' she moaned softly.

Kate leapt up and rushed to her, grabbing her by the shoulders. 'Are you sure, Bess? Are you sure?' she cried, trying to beat down the rising panic inside her.

'The merchant below, babbling in his ale, said there had been an attempt to steal the Crown Jewels this very morning, and the robbers have been captured and thrown into the Tower. Oh Kate, what are we to do now?'

Bess covered her face with her hands and sobbed. 'Oh Colonel!' she wailed, 'to think of you brought so low! Oh Kate, they'll cut off his head for sure!' She threw herself on a chair and wept noisily.

Kate tried to soothe her, for fear Mistress Millichope and the others would hear and come running.

'Hush, Bess, hush! We must think. We must plan how we may try to rescue them.'

Bess looked up with a sneer. 'From the Tower? No man alive has ever escaped from that place, and you are a fool to think it. No, no, he's done for this time!'

She howled again into the hem of her gown. Kate turned away and began pacing the room again. She cared little now what became of Blood, but Tom too had been taken prisoner, it seemed, and she must try to think of some way to help him.

'Were they all taken, Bess?' she asked.

'Yes – but for Holloway, if the news is true.'

Kate still hoped. Rumour was a fickle wench and it could yet be true that only some, if any, of the robbers had been caught. Tom might reappear still, mayhap sneaking home furtively in the middle of the night.

But although Kate sat up all night, waiting for the slightest sound of a footstep or creak on the stairs, Tom did not come.

James, Duke of Ormond, stood in the library of Clarendon House and felt well-pleased with himself. In the spring warmth his aching bones did not trouble him so severely, and the pale sunshine illuminated the panelled walls and well-filled book-shelves of his study which he loved so well. But this morning the letters and dispatches on his desk were neglected. He had another more pleasing matter to occupy his mind.

He gazed out of the mullioned window at the trees below, and recalled how the sight reminded him of the view from his window at Dublin Castle. It was on a spring morning such as this – how long ago now? Eight years – how time flew! On just such a morning he had looked down and watched and waited for Blood to attack the Castle, and later when the attempt had failed and Blood had somehow slipped through his fingers, he had sworn never to rest until he had the audacious fellow clapped in prison.

Eight years had passed, and unceasingly the fellow had continued to plague him, even daring to kidnap him from his own coach not five months ago! But patience was its own reward. Although Ormond had not the satisfaction of having captured the malefactor himself, he was filled with pleasure at the newly-arrived piece of intelligence. Blood had been taken, trying to steal the Crown Jewels, confound his impertinence! and was even now languishing in the Tower.

Buckingham would be far from pleased, thought Ormond, chuckling at the thought. It was almost certain it was he who had put the villain up to the kidnapping attempt on Ormond last December. He had no doubt had the fellow in his pay for countless other nefarious activities too, and now he had lost a most capable lieutenant. Ormond smiled as he recalled his son's anger over the kidnapping incident, and how he had accused Buckingham before the King himself. He was a young man of courage, Lord Ossory, if a trifle impetuous.

Indeed, Ormond was highly pleased with the day's events. He liked Buckingham no better than Buckingham liked him, and he was looking forward to seeing his discomfiture over Blood when next they met at Whitehall.

Blood was committed to the Tower under a warrant made out to the Governor, Sir John Robinson, on the grounds of outlawry for treason. Hunt and Parrett's warrants were for dangerous crimes and practices. All London throbbed with the news of their daring attempt, from the glittering corridors of Whitehall to the most evil, foetid alley of Southwark. The sensational news drove every other topic of conversation from people's minds, and speculation was rife as courtier and courtesan hazarded guesses as to the reason for Blood's audacious attempt.

Blood, Hunt and Parrett were brought for examination first before Sir Gilbert Talbot, the Provost-Marshal, and then before Dr Chamberlain and Sir William Waller, but each man refused obstinately to speak. Sir John Robinson tried threats, but in vain.

'Do your worst,' said Blood composedly, 'I shall speak to none but His Majesty himself.'

'His Majesty?' Sir John repeated in surprise.

'That is so. To none but the King himself.'

The consternation caused by Blood's

words had the desired effect. Within days Sir John reported to Blood that His Majesty was 'desirous of seeing so bold a ruffian,' and consequently an interview had been arranged for Blood at Whitehall.

Blood smiled contentedly. It was not altogether surprising that the King had agreed, for he had been known to conduct interrogations before, and had proved himself quite a master of examination. Blood muttered a few words to Hunt as they passed, heavily manacled, in a Tower corridor.

'Bear up, lad. I'm to see the King. We'll find ourselves free yet,' he murmured.

A few days later Sir John sent Blood to Whitehall. He was afraid to send him in a coach, however well-guarded, for fear that Blood's confederates would raid the coach and rescue their leader, so instead he sent him under guard by water. From the Tower stairs the wherry plied swiftly up river, the musketeers around Blood watching the river banks warily for any sign of interference.

At Whitehall he was taken ashore and across the great courtyard into the Palace. After waiting some time in an ante-room he was led at last into the royal presence.

King Charles sat on a gilded chair, raised

from the floor on a low dais. He sat lazily, his tall, lithe figure draped rather than sitting on the chair, but his rich velvet tunic and breeches made him a handsome, imposing figure nonetheless. He watched curiously as Blood was marched in, but his fingers continued to caress the small spaniel dog which lay in his lap. Alongside the King stood the small, slender figure of his latest mistress, the fair-haired French maid, Louise Keroualle, the translucent whiteness of her skin acting as a foil to the swarthy, dark features of the King.

All round His Majesty stood many courtiers, all elegantly-dressed and glittering with jewels, and beyond them a rank of soldiers, the royal bodyguard. Blood looked about him, and his face was dark with displeasure.

The chattering ceased as Blood neared the throne, his hands still manacled behind him. Every eye was straining to see this legendary creature about whom all London was buzzing. The Duke of Ormond stood erect, his old face creased into a smile while Buckingham stood glowering angrily.

Blood stood at last before the dais, his head held high and his dark eyes glaring defiantly at the King.

'Well now,' the King's voice drawled lazily, 'so this is the man who would wear my crown?'

'Not I, Sire.' Blood's voice was low but the force in it carried it to every part of the vast chamber. 'I would not wear a crown upon my head, for it carries too much care and responsibility for one man.'

'That it does,' the King agreed amiably. 'Then why did you attempt to steal it?'

Blood stood silent. The King waited patiently for a moment, then began again. The courtiers were growing restless. 'Well? Did you not request an interview here in order to plead your cause? Silence will advance your cause not a jot. Have you naught to say to us?'

Lord Ossory stepped forward from among the courtiers. Ormond clicked his tongue impatiently. He hoped his son was not going to utter some rash, ill-considered words once again.

'Sire,' said Ossory, 'I beg you waste no more time on this fellow, for his crimes are manifold. He it was who tried to kill my father, and for that alone he should die! Hang him at once, and have done with the malefactor!'

'Patience, Ossory, and let us hear what the

man has to say,' the King murmured, but Buckingham strode forward.

'Your Majesty, this man can be of more use to us alive than dead. I beg you may show your mercy and pardon him, for I could use him well.'

'No doubt of that,' Ossory muttered angrily.

'Curb your tongue, sir.' The King spoke sharply this time. 'Well, Blood, have you naught to say?'

Blood looked him full in the face. 'I have much to say, Your Majesty, but it is for your ear alone. I did not think to have to speak of private matters before all your ministers and courtiers. I understood I was to have a private audience, with you alone.'

Tongues began buzzing at the man's temerity, but the King rose lazily, put the dog aside, and motioned the court to be silent. 'Then so you shall,' he said quietly, and walked towards the door. His ministers hastened to him, to warn him of the danger, but he brushed them aside coolly. 'The man was once a stout, bold fellow in the royal service, for so my cousin Rupert has declared, and for that if no other reason I shall grant him what he seeks. Stand aside and let me pass.'

Outside the great chamber the King paused and waited for Blood to follow, closely escorted by his guards.

'Unchain him,' the King commanded peremptorily, 'for I cannot speak freely with a man who is bound.'

The soldiers looked uncertainly at each other for a moment, then did as they were told. After all, orders from a king outweighed those of a mere officer. Satisfied, the King led Blood into a smaller but no less ornate chamber. He sat down at a long oaken table and motioned Blood, who was standing just within the double doors, to come and sit opposite him. His dark, handsome face creased into a mischievous smile as Blood seated himself stiffly.

'Well now, Blood, I have the pleasure of meeting the greatest villain in my country face to face and alone. Will you speak freely with me now?'

'Gladly, Sire. But I am not the greatest villain. There are many surrounding you with friendly faces who scheme far worse against you than I have ever done.'

'I do not doubt it. But how have you ever proved your love and loyalty to me? You have wrought naught but destruction and dissension for my ministers for many a year.

Was it not you who thought to seize His Grace the Duke of Ormond and Dublin Castle? Was it not you who rescued Mason at York? And again you tried to kidnap Ormond only last Christmas?'

'Aye, Sire. I did all these things. Yet once I had Your Majesty at my mercy, and I spared your life.' Blood said the words coolly and watched the King's dark eyebrows rise. He told him then of the misty morning on the Battersea shore, when Blood had stayed the pistols of his confederates.

'Why should you have planned to take my life, Blood? And why then did you change your mind?' The King's equable tone of voice on hearing of his near escape Blood noted with approval. The King was a man of courage like himself.

'I had no loyalty to the Crown of England, Sire. I fought for the King your father once, but when the war was over your Lord Lieutenant in Ireland robbed me of all my lands and made me a pauper. My wife lives in hardship, continually ill, and I have been driven to desperate deeds to right my wrongs.'

'Why then, if you felt so aggrieved against the monarchy, did you not take your opportunity and shoot me?'

'I could not, Sire. There was that in your manner and your bearing which filled me with respect and love for you. I could no more harm you than you could harm your bitch there.' Blood indicated the spaniel at the King's feet, nuzzling her master affectionately. She must have followed the King from the great chamber unnoticed, and the King was absentmindedly stroking her head as he spoke.

His Majesty smiled understandingly. 'And what is your explanation for the attempted theft of my Crown Jewels, Blood? What report are we to issue to the world for your action? Some say that you were put up to it by one of my nobles, a discontent who would have the crown for himself. Is it to be broadcast that you were securing the regalia on his behalf?'

Blood smiled to himself. He knew that the King was referring to Buckingham and that that duke was ambitious and impetuous enough to attempt just such a deed. Doubtless the King knew too of the many secret exchanges of letters between Blood and Buckingham and that Blood had acted on Buckingham's behalf before now.

'It's a possible explanation, Sire, but one which would only bring trouble and discredit on your ministry.'

'Buckingham's defence of you, openly, here in Court, would give credence to the tale,' the King reminded him.

'He seeks to save me only that he may use me to his own ends on other occasions,' Blood countered.

'And to spite Ormond,' the King added. 'But it is true you could be useful to the government, for you could discover for us what we cannot uncover for ourselves.'

'Spy for you?' Blood murmured. 'Indeed, I could be of use to you in that way, I imagine.'

'But to the matter in hand,' pursued the King. 'What other explanation can there be for your theft?'

'For money – my own personal gain,' Blood answered. 'The value of the jewels would have made me a rich man for the rest of my days if I had got clean away.'

The King leaned back in his chair and laughed loudly and merrily. 'Oh, Blood,' he gasped, 'the gold and jewels in my regalia are but counterfeit, did you not know that? The few miserable pounds you would have raised from them would not have lasted you beyond one rowdy night in a bawdy house.'

Blood was regarding him in astonishment.

'Is this true? I risked so much – for so little? No, I do not believe you. You are cozening me, are you not?'

The King's dark eyes twinkled. 'Now you will never know, my brave Colonel. And it was a brave, if somewhat foolhardy, attempt. There are many other rumours circulating London too, as to why you stole my jewels.'

'What are they?'

'That you were bribed to do it by the treasurers of my navy, in an attempt to pay off the massive debt I owe my sailors.'

'Ah!' Blood tapped his long nose knowingly. 'Now that is an explanation which has a ring of truth about it. Everyone knows how depleted Your Majesty's coffers have become as a result of your generosity to loyal royalists and to – others for their favours.'

'My mistresses, you mean,' the King murmured. 'It is true I am in want of money, but not so badly as to have my treasurers rob me of my jewels. And then there is the rumour which is circulating the Court here,' the King added after a pause, 'which my courtiers find the most titillating of all.'

'And what is that, may I ask, Sire?'

'That I put you up to the theft myself, Blood.'

Blood's bushy eyebrows rose high on his forehead. 'You, Sire? 'Tis a most unworthy thought in the minds of those who profess to love you well. But to what end?'

'So that you might take the jewels abroad and pawn or sell them for me, to rescue me from my penury,' the King replied, leaning forward on the table to look Blood full in the face. 'Now what do you say to that explanation?'

'Small use that would be if the jewels were counterfeit, Sire.'

'As you say, Blood, *if* they were counterfeit.'

There was a long silence between the two men, each regarding the other with an air that was full of unspoken meaning. Then the King sat slowly upright.

'I am to judge what is to be done with you, Blood. What if I should grant you your life?'

Blood looked at him proudly. 'I should endeavour to deserve it, Your Majesty,' he replied.

'Well said. I take it we shall have no more trouble from you or your comrades then?'

'None, I assure you, Sire. Henceforth I shall devote myself entirely to your service, and your clemency will render your name even more beloved than before.'

'Enough,' said the King sharply. 'You speak more like a practised courtier than a loyal soldier. All I require from you is that you live peaceably and cause my ministers no more grey hairs. Will you settle in London or return to Ireland?'

Blood spread his hands expressively. 'Whither should I return in Ireland, Sire? My estate in Sarney is no longer mine.'

'It shall be returned to you, and a pension of five hundred a year and a place at Court if you so desire.'

Blood bowed his head in acknowledgement. 'Your Majesty is most gracious,' he murmured.

'That will content you?'

'I should like my comrades to be pardoned also, Sire.'

The King clicked his tongue. 'So they shall, Blood, but in due course. It would appear most odd if you are freed and handsomely recompensed and your fellow-conspirators also. But soon, I promise, they too shall be free.'

'Than I am content, Sire, and deeply grateful.'

The King pushed the spaniel aside and rose, crossing to the window that overlooked the river. 'There is one other matter,

Blood,' he said, standing with his broad back turned to the Colonel. 'What story will the world hear of our encounter today?'

'None, Sire. None from me. I shall ever hold my tongue.' Blood rose to his feet.

The King turned. 'What will they think has passed between us, I wonder. They are awaiting a public execution of a traitor, and will explode with amazement when I pardon you.'

Blood smiled. 'I shall never breathe a word, Sire, so you may put about what story you will.'

'I would prefer to give no explanation.'

'Then I shall lay such a cloud of dust about me that none shall ever know the truth of the matter,' Blood assured him. 'You can rely upon me utterly, Sire, for I am your man.'

The King smiled contentedly and bent to pick up the spaniel. 'Then let us return to my ministers. You will be sent back to the Tower, but have no fear, very soon you will be freed, and your comrades likewise.'

NINETEEN

The days dragged by in an agony of despair for Kate. News filtered through Alsatia, many distorted tales changed by the ever-gossiping tongues, but at last it became clear that both Tom and the Colonel were held prisoners in the Tower. Rumours of Blood securing an interview with the King filled the taverns, but it seemed he had been thrown back into the Tower and hope for his life was fading fast.

Kate was sickened by the talk. Erstwhile admirers of the Colonel now babbled excitedly about the public execution which would undoubtedly be laid on for their entertainment, and speculation grew as to how many others of his friends might be taken and punished.

But no constables came to Alsatia in their search. The vile criminal inhabitants continued to pursue their way of life unmolested. Kate tried desperately to beg Bess to find Holloway or some others of Blood's conspirators, in an attempt to plan some means of rescuing him and Tom, but Bess shook her head despairingly and said it was useless.

Kate fretted and pined. Silken May sunshine warmed into June and then blazed into July, and by now even Alsatia's denizens were beginning to forget the promised execution which seemed somehow to have been overlooked. There were many visitors to London and the pickings were too plentiful for pickpockets and prostitutes to concern themselves unduly with a former friend now fallen on hard times. Even Bess, with the resilience born of long years of disappointment, soon dried her eyes and turned back to her work in the inn. Only Kate remembered and wept.

Blood himself, lying in a filthy dungeon with no other companion but the rats, might have been forgiven for thinking he had been forgotten. He was not even allowed to see Hunt or Parrett. A week after his visit to Whitehall he had written a letter to the King.

'May it please Your Majesty these may tell and inform you that it was Sir Thomas Osborn and Sir Thomas Littleton, both your treasurers for your navy, that set me to steal your crown, but he that feed me with money was James Littleton, Esq. 'Tis he that pays under your treasurer at your Pay Office. He is a very bold, villainous fellow, a very rogue, for I and my companions have had many a hundred pounds of him of your Majesty's money to encourage us upon this attempt. I pray no words of the confession, but know your friends. Not else but am Your Majesty's prisoner and, if life spared, your dutiful subject whose name is Blood, which I hope is not what Your Majesty seeks after.'

Blood sent the letter unsealed so that other eyes might read it, and smiled to think how that would give rise to yet further speculation as to the truth of the matter. True to his word to the King, he spared no effort to cloud the truth as far as he could. The King had still not pardoned him publicly, and Blood would not be safe until he did.

But no answer came to his letter. As the weeks slipped by Blood almost gave up hope, but at last, in July, Lord Arlington came to the Tower with sealed warrants for the Tower Governor, Sir John Robinson.

'Warrants?' said Sir John. 'For Blood's execution?'

'I know not. They are sealed,' Arlington replied. 'Open them and read for yourself.'

Of all this Kate knew nothing. She lay on the truckle bed in her little chamber, listening dully to the gaiety and chatter of Mistress Millichope's clients below, and wondered listlessly what was to become of her.

It was apparent now that she would never see her beloved Tom again. Bess had long ago given up moping and weeping and gone back to her routine work, pleasing Mistress Millichope's more affluent patrons, and Kate too would have to abandon hope and plan life anew. Once she had plucked up courage to leave the safety of Alsatia and cross the bridge to the Tower, in the hope of being allowed to see Tom and bring him food, but the trooper at the gate had turned her away brusquely, telling her that no one had leave to visit a traitor.

What else was there left for her to do, to try to help Tom? He was beyond her reach and her help now, and if gossip was true, he had not long to live. She could not bear to watch him die, like any common horse thief. She would leave London first, but whither could she go, alone and penniless in a strange land?

For Blood Kate felt no pity at all. It was he, with his madcap schemes, who had brought this terrible situation about. What fools they had been, both Tom and herself, to be dazzled by him, to listen to him and fall in with him! If only... But it was too late now.

Mistress Millichope was growing impatient. The Colonel was no longer footing the bill handsomely as he had formerly done, and the landlady had made it clear to Kate that she wanted either payment, and that right soon, or Kate could work for her living in the establishment. The prospect was sickening, and Kate was full of despair as she lay abjectly on her bed.

There was a knock. The old woman was at the door again, leaning on the jamb and wiping her snivelly nose on the hem of her greasy kirtle. 'Well?' she demanded coarsely.

Kate sat up and looked at the old dame. 'Well what, Mistress Millichope?'

'Have yer decided? Can yer pay me or are yer ready to work? The house is full of noisy men tonight, drinking and carousing, and before long they'll all be asking for wenches. Can yer pay what yer owe me, or am I to send one of 'em up to yer?'

Kate sank back on the bed. 'Do as you will,' she said feebly. She no longer cared.

'Then for the Lord's sake pretty yerself up a mite, girl, 'cos there's not a man who'd want a pale, puny thing that looks half-dead. Brush yer hair and pinch yer cheeks, my girl, and do what yer can. The state yer in now, there's no one as'd give more 'n a groat for a tumble with yer.'

The old woman snorted and swept out. Kate lay still, uncaring and unthinking, and after a few moments she rose and began brushing her hair listlessly. What did it matter how she looked? And why should she care now about lying with a man who was a stranger to her?

She sighed as she remembered the times she had lain with Val, even when she did not love him. It had not been too hard then, so why now? Perhaps if she closed her eyes and thought of Tom...

Kate slapped the brush savagely on her hair. No, she must stop thinking of Tom. She must think of him as already dead, gone beyond her reach like her parents were, if she thought of him at all. She must take herself firmly in hand and try to carve out a new life for herself, however degrading it might be to begin.

A footstep sounded on the stair. Kate's brush paused in mid-air as she listened. It was a man's footstep, firm and decisive, just like Tom's used to be. Her heart flinched for a moment at the thought. No, she must not hope. She must abandon all those fantasies. It would be the gentleman client Mistress Millichope had sent up for Kate's services.

The footfalls ceased outside Kate's door, and a knock came, firm but quiet. Kate did not answer. She looked at herself in the cracked mirror and lifted her chin defiantly. She would endure whatever was to come – for the time being.

The knob turned and the door opened. Kate turned slowly, reluctant to see the face of the man she must humour. At the sight of him, tall and broad in the doorway, her breath caught in her throat. In the deceptive half-light of evening he looked exactly like Tom. Her mind was playing wishful tricks on her again! Fiercely she beat down the longing.

'Kate?' The voice was soft and tender, but unmistakably Tom's. Kate's breath escaped in a sob of disbelief, and in a moment he had crossed the little chamber and gathered her to him, crushing her close and murmuring into her ear.

'Oh my Kate! I thought you would be gone! I never thought to find you still here,' he said brokenly.

'You – you asked me to wait for you,' Kate

reminded him in a whisper.

'Oh Kate, my precious Kate!' He was kissing her and murmuring and Kate, disbelieving still, tried hard to hold back the tears. At length she drew him to sit on the stool and she knelt by his side.

'Tell me how you are here, Tom. Did you escape?'

'Escape? No indeed. The King has granted a full pardon to the Colonel and me.'

'A pardon?' Kate could scarcely believe her ears. Everyone in London had them both already condemned and hanged, and it was unbelievable that they were alive – and free!

Tom's eyes gleamed from his hollow face. 'Yes, Kate, is it not incredible? Lord Arlington brought warrants to the Governor that everyone fully expected to be warrants for our execution. Yet miraculously, they contained orders for our release and full pardon. Don't ask me the reason for it, Kate, for I do not know it myself.' He laughed, caressing her cheek with his fingertip. 'For me it suffices that I am free and you are still here waiting for me. From now on we shall never be separated again, I swear it, my Kate.'

'And Blood also is free?' Kate mused aloud. 'It will not be long before you are away on another of his goose-brained schemes then, I fancy.'

'Not I, Kate, for Blood is to live at Court and that is no life for me. I want to settle with you, my dearest, in a house of our own, if you'll have me.'

Kate sighed, unable yet to believe her good fortune. Not only was Tom miraculously restored to her after she had given him up for dead, but he was freed from his slavery to that rogue Blood. She looked up into Tom's gentle eyes, and wondered again.

He looked pale and wan after his weeks of confinement in the Tower but his eyes shone with life and hope. His hands caught hers urgently, and Kate felt the ring on his finger cutting into her palm. She looked at the bloodstone and recalled once again the gipsy's prophecy. She laughed gently.

'I told you once you were the man of courage who was to change my life,' she reminded Tom, 'and you told me then it was not you but the Colonel.'

'Because of the bloodstone ring? Well, it was once his ring,' Tom said, looking down at it thoughtfully.

'*His* ring? But you told me it was given you by your father, did you not?' Kate's voice was shaking.

'I spoke no less than the truth, Kate.'

'You mean – the Colonel is your father?' Kate could not believe the words as she spoke them, and she stared at Tom disbelievingly. He looked at her soberly.

'He is. But his wife is not my mother.'

Kate was utterly bewildered. Why had she not guessed it before? Was it not Tom's resemblance to the Colonel that had first caught her eye in the Pheasant? And it certainly answered why Tom had followed the man with such loving devotion. Tom drew her closer as he went on.

'Blood rarely sees his wife, and as you know, he is no celibate monk when he is away from her. I am his son by one of his early loves, now dead I fear. He has sons by his wife, but he sees little of them. One, Holcroft, ran away to sea at the age of twelve, and I think the Colonel hoped that I would replace him as a loyal and dutiful son, to follow in his footsteps.'

'I see,' Kate murmured. 'Then that is why you followed him blindly into any escapade, without question. I begin to see it all now.'

'You thought me reckless and foolish, enslaved to the charm of an irresistible rogue, eh?' Tom teased her.

'And he is a rogue!' Kate said emphatically. 'He was my hero for many a year, until I met him again and learnt how he behaved.'

'A rogue mayhap he is,' Tom admitted, 'but a courageous and daring man nonetheless, as I'm sure you will agree, my Kate. But he need concern us no longer, for we have done with him. Come, let us pack and go from here as quickly as we may, for we have lingered too long in the haunts of the ungodly as it is.'

He rose and began helping Kate to collect her belongings together. At the doorway Kate paused.

'Strange,' she said reflectively, 'that the Colonel never told us you were his son. One would imagine he would be proud of it.'

Tom grunted. 'Strange mayhap, but there are many secrets Blood keeps to himself. No one, I think, will ever know the full story of that man's life. To the end he will remain an enigma.'

They walked down the narrow flight of stairs.

'Tell me, Tom, did Blood see the King? What happened? How did it come about that you were pardoned?' Kate asked him as he set down her leather case to open the outer door.

Tom laughed, a happy infectious chuckle.

'To those questions, my love, I cannot answer. He saw the King, but what transpired and why we were freed will remain, I think, yet another of Blood's mysteries. I doubt if we shall ever know, but what does it matter now?'

'You are right,' Kate answered gravely. 'Nothing else matters now.'

And taking her hand in his, Tom led her out into the noisy, stinking little alley and away up to the Temple Gardens where London's air was a little purer, and there was peace.

EPILOGUE

Pardons were issued to Thomas Blood and to Thomas Blood, Junior, for 'all treasons, murders, felonies, etc. committed ... from the day of His Majesty's accession to the present', and the Colonel found himself, as the King had promised, once again in possession of his estates, a place at Court, and a pension of five hundred pounds a year from Irish lands.

Blood stayed in London, living in Bowling

Alley, Westminster, and presented himself at Court in Whitehall with complete composure, though he was still hated and feared by many Londoners. He earned his pardon well, giving information on conspirators which led to their being brought to justice. Lord Rochester openly wrote epigrams about Blood 'that wears treason in his face', and many wondered at the King's clemency to such a villain.

He died in August 1680, but even his burial could not quell the fears of many people who believed it could be yet another trick. Only when his grave was re-opened and the body shown to have an unnaturally large thumb were they reassured that at last the old fox was genuinely dead.

This Large Print Book for the partially sighted, who cannot read normal print, is published under the auspices of

THE ULVERSCROFT FOUNDATION